M000206564

# re-ring

**A novel by**

## Russell H. Ford

BOOK
PUBLISHING
CENTER

Amazon Book Publishing Center
420 Terry Ave N, Seattle, Washington,
98109, U.S.A

The opinions expressed by the Author are not necessarily those held by Amazon Book Publishing Center.

Ordering Information: Quantity sales and special discounts are available on quantity purchases by corporations, associations, and others.

For details, contact the publisher at info@amazonbookpublishingcenter.com

Printed in the United States of America.
ISBN: 978-1-915911-21-6 (hardcover)

Amazon Book Publishing Center works with authors, and aspiring authors, who have a story to tell and a brand to build. Do you have a book idea you would like us to consider publishing? Please visit AmazonBookPublishingCenter.com for more information.

*To my one and only Wife: Mollie*
*Forty-three years in September of*
*2019 will still not be enough.*

———————

To my parents, who blessed me with the genetic material to succeed.

To my sisters, who set the bar so very high.

To my extended family, who have endured me. To my friends, who have encouraged, criticized, and challenged me at every turn. To the Boy Scouts of America, they helped educate me in the really important things in life. To the North Thurston School District, Lacey, Washington, where curiosity is encouraged. My Mother was a substitute and full-time teacher there. Rest in peace, Mom.

To the fire service everywhere, especially in Washington State, and specifically the Lacey, Tenino, Lakebay, Seattle, Chelan County District #1, and Pullman fire departments; to Washington Public Power Supply System (Energy Northwest), the Pierce County Fire Marshal's office, the Chelan County Fire Marshal's office, and all fire service training programs. Only firefighters know the truth about the Red Devil.

To law enforcement everywhere, especially in Washington State, and specifically the Thurston, Whitman, Douglas, Chelan, and Pierce County Sheriff's offices and the Lacey, Pullman, Wenatchee, East Wenatchee, Tenino, and Seattle police departments. The Seattle Police Department's SWAT team and shooting range personnel are also worthy of high praise. Thanks to the SWAT Team for honoring me recently. Thanks to David Segarra for putting up with me.

I was told several times that a good writer has a great editor. I was blessed with Cherie Tucker and Kat Dawson.

Plus, there are many people—Jeff; Glenda; Doctors Saint Clair, Card, Ruditzky, West, and Hoffman; Sara; Steven D. Mace; Louis; and more—who read and critiqued. Thanks to Frankie Boyer, Darryl Wayne, and Allan Handelman. Thanks to Amy and Elliott for their kind attentions. Thanks to Russ Davis of Grey Dog Press in Spokane.

To the Craft in Hayward, California, in Hanna, Alberta, Canada, in Kitimat, British Columbia, Canada, in Cameron Parish Louisiana, and in Richland, Washington who kept in contact asking about de-pop, and the sequel. Thanks to Toby and James, and the rest of the WFD-HPC gang, and Wonder Nurse Carrie!

To the Cabo Cantina, Cabo San Lucas, BCS, Mexico, for letting me camp out in Hemingway fashion in the back-dining area with my computer, straw hat, and red bandana as I wrote, rewrote, and made a thousand corrections. Samir and the staff were curious and helpful at every turn. Try the guacamole!

To Doctors R. Phillips, W. Shields, and J. Haynie, who collectively saved me from going blind.

To Jack's, where I met the musician Horacio and Captain Charley!

To Mike Marohn, Senior Vice President at the Marohn Crofts Group at Morgan Stanley, Olympia, Washington, who was my soccer teammate at North Thurston High School and has been my financial advisor for thirty years. If I got there or get there, it was because of you.

Many people have been shocked, that I, the "Author" would let so many people read the final drafts prior to publishing. Many questioned why I would do such a thing? I wanted them to know that I had let others read my book as a 'peer' review, in fact, the first book de-pop was based on medical technology. I had at least five physicians, two Ph.D. chemists-chemical engineers, and a variety of other highly skilled and relevant professionals, including a retired Air Force Intelligence Officer, go over the work to verify that the contents relating to the 'science' were in fact real. It was my job as the writer to take fact, to take the sterility of science and weave a story around and through it, thus blurring the edges of fact and fiction. It was incumbent that the facts had to be right. And thus, was born the committee of Beta Readers.

re-ring required that I expand my Beta Readers from the identified physicians and scientists to the world of religion, and to that end I wish to thank the Abu Bakr Masjid of San Diego, whose staff was most professional and informative, to the only Synagogue in SE Texas, led by the Rabbi Taub. Thanks to the McCain's as well. Thanks to the many family and friends that gave me their personal, sometimes deeply personal, views of their faiths. Thanks to Jamal Rahman of Seattle for our lengthy phone conversation.

Of special note was the diligence and absolute thoroughness of Kat Dawson, my friend whom I worked with in Canada. Kat's take on the editing, proofing, story line, and the nature of the characters should have her listed as 'co-author', which I offered as it seemed more than fair considering her invaluable input. I suspect she is a far better writer than I.

Of special note was the "heart" I had to install in many characters after the review of Carolynn Ferris, whom I am very proud to have known for over three decades.

And to the Beta's that mandated that I resurrect Ruby La Push or be made to suffer for it. I am still taken aback that a fictional character that lived only in my mind had begun to live and breathe in the minds of others. I kindly reflect upon this as a testament to at least getting one thing right in my writing. In retribution, I have brought back your worst fears.

Thanks to my new acquaintances of Mike W and Kelly G at Sabine Pass, who kindly reviewed and commented about the rough draft(s). Tami and Robbie D for their kind support.

Of special note were the help of Fairchild Airforce Base, and the Reserve Units that reside there. Their input was of great value.

Of very special note was the help of the Redhawks, headquartered at Portland International Airport, for the description of their mission and their aircraft. My Father, Lt. Colonel Donald M. Ford, USAF, would have been proud. Rest in Peace, Dad.

Thanks to my brother-in-law Lt. Colonel Jake Bailey, USMC, for his technical input and vast knowledge of the United States Armed Forces.

Thanks to my many acquaintances that are past members of the Canadian Forces who educated me on their unique perspectives on sniper-counter sniper operations, from whom Everett Pierce is based on. I revel in the fact that I am Canadian American!

Thanks to all the members of the Armed Forces that

have worked on projects with me over the years, I am grateful for the input.

Thanks to Dr. Bob Lillie, from Oregon State University who provided guidance on plate tectonics and continental drift; the late Roger Easton of the North Thurston School District, teacher and historian, who first explained the theories to me when I was in the fourth grade.

Thanks to the Kawasaki Motorcycle Company for providing technical guidance, and specifically the sales agents I chatted with from the San Diego area.

Thanks to Jason Bourque, Director, Vancouver, Canada, and Tatiana Turner, Actress and Executive Producer, Vancouver and Los Angeles for their encouragement.

Thanks to the sales staff at Academy Sports on Memorial in Nederland, Texas for technical guidance, and their patience as I picked their brains over M-16's, 300 Blackouts, AR-15's, M-1 Garand's, and more. And Chris T. for his take on firearms, being a devil's advocate, and for me leaning on him. To my friends Ms. T, Mr. Al, Paul and Roger of NCCER, and Les and Dan of T. I. Marilyn and Cynthia along with Tracey, Roxie and Dawn - you rock!

Thanks to my brother-in-law Bob W., for his technical advice on vehicles. You can start on my truck any day now. Skip the nitrous oxide. No, wait, keep it. To Phil and Vivian for creating my Wife, Mollie. Rest in Peace, Phil. For my sisters-in-law, Carol, Bobbie, Jennie, Vicki, and Traci; and brothers-in-law George and Ron.

Thanks to the redoubtable Alison Bailey, beauty and talent in one package, you might think of her as the Author's Ravenna Lakota.

The challenge to you all: I have an excellent memory.

I photocopy everyone; your actions, your reactions, facial expressions, strengths, weaknesses, humor, sorrow, anger, patience, and more, so much more. From a mere snippet of overheard conversation at a coffee shop, idle chatter in line at the supermarket, or in the middle of a million-dollar meeting, I record, I remember. Like my new friends at the Johnson Bayou Library, and the dear and sweet D2 and Sherry! To our friend Kathleen Huffman at the Metaline Falls Library, it was only a matter of time before we connected!

If I have seen you, or heard you, you are in here. That should be . . . worrying.

R. Ford
6/13/2019
Richland, WA

# Preface

I spend a long time thinking about the world. Yes, I stand in awe on starry nights looking into the heavens thinking about how small I really am. Like most humans I spend a few moments asking the "What if" questions.

Setting the overarching religious aspects aside for a moment, we can look to the Theory of Continental Drift and Plate Tectonics. After having survived earthquakes in California, Washington, Canada, and Japan, I can tell you that the earth *moves*. Ample geologic evidence exists that the continents did drift apart from one another over Earth's lifespan.

There are questions, mercifully, that have not been answered: How did the Pyramids get built? How did supposedly ancient and technologically disadvantaged civilizations move massive blocks of stone from one place to another, on virtually every continent, that all oddly sprang from a single massive continent? What is the link? And where are the devices that allowed this to happen? Why is it that *every* civilization that created these structures have all faded away? If the cranes, bulldozers, and cement mixers were left in the desert sun near Hoover Dam, they would still be there. Why it is that none of the machinery that built the other structures has been found is stunning, and most curious. We must ask these questions or be doomed to melancholy recitation of the theories of others.

As the son of a noted Washington State geologist, I too, looked into the history of the planet. From the theories of the creation of the universe, to how our smallish solar system makes up a very tiny speck of an immense arm of a massive galaxy, and to the endless nature of however far it is the edge of the time; I rather keep my focus on Planet Earth.

While not an *un*-believer in aliens, I tend to rely on what I can see and lay my hands on or talk to people that have. For one, I am grateful that mysteries exist. What a dull and drab existence we would have to face if there were not things to *solve*. I am endlessly amused by the notion of us looking for extraterrestrials, when in fact, are we not extraterrestrials to some other planet?

The religious aspects of the Creation Theory have always fascinated me, and yet to some degree they are remarkably the same. Some beliefs are held that God, the Creator, the Eternal Spirit, the Supreme Being, created and re-created the world and the entire universe on multiple occasions. In my research I have talked to Evangelicals, Ministers, Priests, Native Americans, Canadian First Nations, Baptists, Jews, Catholics, those of the Islamic faith, and even Snake Handlers. At the end of each interview I have asked the same question:

How do we know this is not an edition of the Universe that gets recreated today, tomorrow, or a week from now, and what could we do to prevent it?

The answer has been remarkably, fantastically, and incredibly similar:

"That is why we pray."
And I for one encourage them to continue.

There are at least two natural preservatives on the planet, the oxygen deprived depths of the oceans, and *ice*.

R. Ford, Richland, WA 7-30-2017

# 1

Neah Bey watched the ant slowly work its way down his arm. The ant stopped and waved its enormous antennas to and fro, sampling its environment. The rain had stopped falling; however, the water still dripped from the eighty feet of jungle canopy overhead that collected the rain. Drops collected into leaves, leaves dripped onto bromeliads, bromeliads gave their water up to vines, and vines let fall small rivulets of water earthward.

For being an uninhabited area of Central American jungle, it was noisy. The water falling created the background noise, as did the birds, insects, various frogs, and other denizens of the night that called, cried, hooted, croaked, screamed, and more.

He hoped the ant would just move peacefully on. As if the little creature heard him, it clacked its massive mandibles together. Sadly, like the last five, it stopped winding its way down his arm and then nipped a bit of flesh. With its prize safely secured in the massive jaws, it scurried away, surely informing all one billion of its kin that a snack bar waited underneath the towering kapok tree.

The night vision monocular was getting heavier with each passing minute. Still he waited; he knew what he had heard was not natural to the rainforest. The sound had come from off to his left. He remained in the darkest shadows of the tree's massive buttressed roots and dangling vines. Water in every form and from every elevation vaporized into a thick mist.

Between the humidity, a multitude of bug bites, the stream of drips, the sweat running in his eyes, and the trek

1

through the jungle on and off the game trails, he was as miserable as he had ever been. Another ant took a nip from his arm. Okay, he thought, *now* I'm as miserable as I have ever been. Until two more ants crawled off the tree roots and marched down his arm.

The scope was kept moving smoothly in a circular pattern. The motion of the optic as it moved with the falling water and slight breeze emulated a large broadleaf in front of him.

Several of the bushes rustled and then parted right in front of him. A tapir moved through the underbrush, causing him to tense. He centered the scope on the large rodent-like ears. They would be better than his in deciphering the jungle noise. The ears twitched in sync with the cries of various critters, front to back and side to side. Then they stopped and began ranging in one direction only. Other night noises did not change the attitude of the ears. The large eyes rolled around in their reflected demon glow in the scope. Slowly lowering its head, the tapir moved silently to his right, the ears still pointed back and to the left.

Freezing into a solid mass, he held the scope steady. Tendrils of mist and fog drifted through the jungle, causing his eyes to dart from place to place, trying to discern real from imagined threats. He saw the slight color shift in the haze. The night vision scope detailed a lower leg, then a hip, and then the muzzle of a rifle.

Slowly he adjusted the aim of the heavy .45. His adversary crouched under a large shrub and began using a night-vision, rifle-mounted scope to survey the area. Bey closed his left eye to prevent being blinded when he took the shot. From under the kapok tree a flash of light and

2

roar divided the night. He darted to the right three steps and hunched down. Echoes of the blast rolled around the jungle and faded away. Gasps of pain, first loud, and then softer, finally fading to labored breathing, which was soon eclipsed by the return of the jungle noises.

He waited. He brought the scope up and began scanning the area again, just in case someone else was as good as or better than he. Satisfied that he was now alone, he stepped forward. Slowly. He held the scope hooked under the bottom of the extended gun hand and examined the prone figure before him. Camo paint and clothing; good boots, somewhat worn; a customized AK with thumbhole stock and a night vision scope, most likely Czechoslovakian, much like his hand-held unit.

He stepped on the barrel of his adversary's gun and placed the muzzle of the .45 against his enemy's temple briefly. The half open eyes did not move. Already the ants were swarming the exposed face and neck. He gave a quick pat down of the corpse and found a small waterproof bag, similar to what white-water rafters and surfboarders use to carry their wallets and car keys. It held a single piece of paper folded into thirds.

Shielding the paper under a large leaf, he slowly unfolded it, already knowing what it would be.

He cursed softly, "Damn, and damn again."

Neah Bey, agent of the under-government of the United States of America, was sixty-five miles south of the Panamanian border in northwest Columbia on Valentine's Day holding a picture of himself. Out of respect he closed the dead man's eyes.

## 2

The radio shack operator tracked them down and showed considerable umbrage about having to walk over in the cold to where Captain Malaga and Lieutenant Bucoda quartered.

"Hey, this isn't like home!" The radio operator scowled, "I have to handle all the radio transmissions day and night, and I don't like being ordered to be a delivery boy!"

Malaga stood up, "Okay, I'm sorry about your working conditions. On the other hand, just what are you talking about?"

"Here!" And with that the operator handed Malaga a sheet of paper with hundreds of four-digit number sequences on it. "You have any idea the time it takes to receive and then repeat back all this crap?"

Malaga took the paper and studied it for a moment. "Again, I am sorry." His eyes traced down the page. "And you said these have been verified?"

"Yes, it took 45 minutes to receive and an hour and a half to repeat back! Got any idea how far behind this puts us? Any idea at all?" the operator challenged.

"As a guess, how about two hours and fifteen minutes?" Bucoda put his feet up on the desk. He smiled at the operator.

"I'll take it upstairs to see if I have to do this work for you people!" And with that the operator stormed out.

"Do you have to antagonize everyone with, what is it? Oh, yeah, the truth." Malaga slapped Bucoda's feet off the table. "Now grab that note pad over there."

Bucoda reached for the note pad and thumbed

through it until he arrived at a page equal to three times the day's date. "Okay, start talking." He took out a pencil and a clean sheet of paper. Bucoda's job was to the do the math calculations from the one sheet and enter the decryption on the other. He waited for Malaga to speak the numbers so he could put the number in the correct box.

Malaga sat back and began reciting each number string.

It took a while to go through all two hundred and ten sets of numbers. At the end Bucoda handed the translation to Malaga. "Looks like we need to start packing for a camping trip."

The wind howled around the building, and ice particles struck the outside. "Yup, these are the orders. Well then, I guess I had better go over to the Admin's office and request our gear." Malaga stood and stretched.

"Great. Gee, am I excited to head out in this weather or what? How cold is it today?" The sarcasm was thick as Bucoda began to sort through his trunk. He laid two Smith and Wesson K-38 revolvers and a box of bullets on the table. "Like they say in the Boy Scouts, 'Be prepared.'"

Malaga frowned at the guns. "I would like to think we won't need those where we are going." He opened his outer jacket and put on a shoulder holster. Into that he slid one of the guns.

"Yeah, me too, and I hope you have been practicing. A lot." Bucoda emphasized the point by rubbing his left upper arm.

"Still whining about that? It's not like you are the only one I've shot." He took a handful of bullets and placed those in his pocket. "I mean, you know, by accident. Sort of." Malaga smiled.

"Ah! The truth comes out, finally!" Bucoda laid two Marine Corp K-Bars on the table, each of the long blades protected in a black leather sheath. "Maybe you should carry just a knife this time. I have reached the conclusion that standing directly in front of you is the safest place to be when you are shooting."

"Hey, I may have saved your life with that shot." Malaga took the long knife from the sheath and spun it in his hands. Bucoda looked at Malaga with a questioning frown. "Just think, you were in the hospital getting patched up, and you could have been hit by a car or something if you weren't." With great skepticism on his face Bucoda gave Malaga the finger.

A gust of wind shook their quarters; groans came from the wood and steel structural members.

"Well, look at it this way, considering the weather and where we have to go and what we have to do, spending a few days in the hospital might seem actually pleasant." The wind abruptly changed directions and shook the structure violently. "Then again, maybe not."

They were young, tough, educated, and scarcely out of their teens. And like everyone they worked with, they just knew each other's names and nothing more. When asked, they worked for an environmental training group out of Washington, D.C., which is what they were told to say. They knew different. Their power chain was far more direct, stopping in the Oval Office with scant few links in between. Their commanding officers were all named Smith.

## 3

Neah accepted the phone call and activated the scrambling device. A series of clicks and chirps faintly assailed his ears. Most of his communications were over regular land lines, so this must be a far more important call to warrant such extra effort.

"Mr. Bey?" asked a female voice.

Neah smiled, it was always the same, even after logging on, using the biometric thumb print device, and they still asked if it was him.

"Yes, this is Bey."

Once he thought it would be funny to answer "Domino's Pizza!" Just once. At the time he thought it was funny. He did not repeat it ever again; others in his organization failed to see the humor in his joke.

The voice said, "Please stand by; Mr. Smith will be with you shortly." Neah had long since gotten over being placed on hold. It was just the way things were.

"Mr. Bey?" a voice asked.

Neah sighed and said, "Yes, this is Neah Bey." There was a small pause, and Bey thought he could hear some papers being rustled in the background.

"Mr. Bey, report to Smith, LLC, immediately. A car will be by shortly; a plane is already waiting for you at Boeing Field. See you upon your arrival around midnight." The line went dead.

Bey sat back in his chair. Only once before had he been so summoned to the head office. In the end, several people he liked and admired died. He had many bitter memories and the occasional bad dream.

Ione simply nodded her head and helped him pack an overnight bag. They kissed and hugged in the front room until the driveway sensor activated, followed shortly by the crunch of tires on the gravel drive.

Ione used the closed-circuit camera system to zoom in on the car and the driver. A hidden camera in the ivy covering the stone wall of the inner drive revealed the driver quite clearly. This driver had been to the house before. The driver pulled out her photo ID and directed it toward the supposedly hidden camera.

Smiling, Ione said, "Rather cheeky don't you think?"

Bey looked at the monitor and said, "Cheeky? Pan down to her rump so I can give you an accurate--" He ducked as Ione attempted to backhand him. Bey circled his arms around his wife and said, "Never fear, I only have eyes for you."

They kissed again, and Ione hugged Bey. "You'd better, or you'll be sleeping in the woodshed," and with a sinister smile, "or be buried under it." They laughed, took one last kiss, and Bey walked to the waiting car. He waved from the rear seat. It was early dusk on a cloudy winter day in the Pacific Northwest.

Euripides the Wonder Cat stuck his nose around the edge of the door. Ever mindful of his magnificent fur and large plume for a tail, he inspected the out of doors. A drop of rain landed on his fur, and he retreated into the house, miffed as only the most spoiled of cats can be. Ione smiled at the seventeen-pound cat and said, "My, aren't we a little prissy?" Euripides sat down with his back to Ione and began cleaning the offending rain drop from his fur.

Bey looked around the back seat of the car for the usual envelope that would contain his briefing papers.

He looked quizzically into the rear view mirror. The driver, a stocky brunette woman of indeterminate age, looked back. She shrugged her shoulders as a way of responding and shifted her attention back to her driving.

Traffic was light, and they made good time from southwest Washington to Boeing Field at the southern edge of Seattle. Waiting for them off Perimeter Road was a Gulfstream jet, highly modified. The driver had phoned ahead and given the crew an estimated time of arrival; the engines were already spinning, and wheel chocks removed.

Bey walked to the plane's built-in stairs and turned to wave good bye to the driver; however, she was already pulling away. He entered the plane and set his bag down on the nearest seat. As before, he was the only passenger in the aircraft. The plane's speaker system carried a message from one of the crew.

"Mr. Bey, please retract the stairs, close the door, and prepare for takeoff."

Bey did as instructed; the plane was already taxiing for the runway. He had been on similar plane rides before. *No-Frills Airline*, he called it. Fortunately, they had left the lavatories unlocked, and he could find water and snacks in the galley. A friend had given him several audio files, and with ear buds in place, he reclined the seat and tried to relax. The flight was uneventful; they arrived in Washington, D.C., at the appointed hour.

By looking at his watch, Bey figured this flight had broken about every law that ever existed for supposedly civilian aircraft. They must have nudged the forbidden zone of the sound barrier the entire way across America. An armored Suburban picked him up at the airport and took him to Smith, LLC.

## 4

Perry smiled through the undergrowth and nodded his head at Randall. It was a signal borne of familiarity. Randall winked back and faded from view. Perry crouched and closed in on the camp from the east. He did not care about a lot of things going on around him; he was focused on the prize. A dog barked and scurried out of the camp headed God knows where. Some birds fluttered around and settled down on the branches directly overhead. Had he been so inclined, he could have reached up and grabbed one from its perch.

His camouflage was complete, head to toe. From time to time he stopped, frozen into position as some motion caught his eye. Perry used the sides of his eyes to scan left and right, never moving too much of his body, as that might draw attention. He skillfully kept trees and bushes between him and the small fire. It took three hours to move one hundred yards undetected.

Now he was obscured by the smoke and the mist that drifted through the forest. He was one with the forest and waited. Voices could be heard from the small camp. He could just make out some of the words.

Perry and Randall had one target, everyone else was secondary. "Gravy" they called the extras. Randall's favorite expression was "The more, the merrier, and the more, the fewer." It was an inside joke, the more they killed or captured, the more interesting the mission, and if they were good, there would be fewer bad actors in the world.

Perry waited; they were already listening to the radio traffic. An incoming message was directed to one individual in the camp, and one only. With that many voices, there was going to be some "gravy."

Two men walked out of the nearest tent and threw some wood on the fire, making it blaze up a little. One carried a sophisticated radio with a two-foot-tall, rubber-coated antenna. At the appointed hour the radio squawked. The first man carrying the radio passed it over to the other.

Randall placed his first arrow into the first man's kidney. It was not really a killing shot in the short term. The man screamed and collapsed on to the ground. Perry's first arrow struck the other man's foot; the tip was designed to deliver a very painful strike and then release an incapacitating agent, which did not prevent that man from screaming as well.

A man dashed out of each of the tents, guns drawn, and were instantly brought down. There was no screaming from them. Five men lay silent on the forest floor. The tips of those arrows exploded when inside the humans. Randall ghosted from the scrub from one side of the camp and Perry from the other, bows drawn. Few others on the planet were skilled enough, practiced enough, strong enough to hold 85-pound draws for as long as they could. Perry directed his nocked arrow and aimed at the chest of the man holding the radio with a failing grip. Randall pulled out a picture and compared it with the one man loosely holding the radio and showed it to Perry. Perry nodded and stepped back.

Both stricken men followed Perry with their eyes. It was Randall that launched an arrow into the chest of the man with the arrow in his kidney. A slight thump could be heard as the arrowhead detonated.

Randall and Perry then turned their attention to the

man that was drugged. The incapacitated man attempted to writhe away. Arms did not respond; legs failed to get traction. Even as the drugs coursed through his system the man's eyes darted from Perry to Randall and back again.

They had a list of questions about people, and places, and other things. Effects of the drug only immobilized the man; it did nothing to deaden the pain. The fire became very handy in helping them extract information. Ultimately the stricken man did not survive his condition.

Sometimes black ops take place in distant foreign lands, sometimes in the remote parts of the Everglades.

## 5

Maybe it was the late hour, maybe it was something else. For the first time in his career as an agent of the grey government, Bey sat alone at midnight in one of the offices off the entry way. It was a plain office, just walls, simple wood floor, a modest desk with a thick glass top, and a straight-backed wooden chair for him to sit on and wait.

After fifteen minutes a lock clicked and a door opened. A slender woman entered the room, a woman he had seen before. She was at the funeral of a mutual friend at the end of a very bad mission. She cast a brief and thin smile at Bey and sat down.

"Thank you for coming on such short notice. We have much to discuss." Mrs. or Miss or Ms. Smith touched the surface of the desk. Without looking up she asked, "Are you familiar with E period L period E period?"

Bey frowned and said, "E-L-E? Extinction Level Event?

I have heard the term, generally in poorly written science fiction."

Mrs. Smith looked up and lost her smile. "It is no longer science fiction; of that I can assure you."

The expressionless features of her face and the voice completely devoid of inflection or even life was disturbing to Bey. He stared into the emotionless grey blue eyes of Mrs. Smith and felt his core muscles tense. She then related events and facts that shook him deeply.

On the ride back to the airport he suggested to the driver to pull over to an all-night convenience store where he could buy a six pack of something. The driver protested and said, "Are you crazy, in this neighborhood?"

Bey said, "If you knew what I knew, you'd join me." The driver declined, but she pulled her side arm and placed extra magazines within reach. It was not the best of neighborhoods.

## 6

Ione became concerned about Neah after the third day. Three days Bey had sat in his chair, stared out into the woods and pasture surrounding their house and scarcely engaged in any conversation at all. He took several walks along the tree line at random times of the day and night. Bey stopped frequently at the memorials he had created out of basalt obelisks for friends he and Ione had lost. Ione could see him sitting on the roughhewn handmade bench next to the obelisks. He seemed to be oblivious to the winter rains pelting him as he sat. Once he came back from a walk, and Ione thought he may have had tears in his eyes.

When the house was built, then re-built, Bey had installed wiring, phone and internet lines to a small room over the woodshed and shop building. It was not only his work space, but also a sanctuary of sorts, more so after his return from Smith, LLC. If he was not on a walk, he could be seen pecking at his laptop computer.

Ione made up a small tray that had a half a sandwich, avocado and cheese, one of Bey's favorites, along with a handful of chips and a diet pop. She got to the door of the wood-shed and could hear Bey shouting on the phone. Ione left the tray on a workbench near the stairs and returned to the house.

She considered calling a mutual friend of theirs, a fellow operative of Neah's, but thought better of it. She had faith, although currently a little shaken, that Neah could rise above most anything. Mr. Morley, a rescued cat, cuddled up next to her for a rub-down of his plump belly. The large cat's purring and kneading action on her thigh comforted Ione Bey, wife of an agent of the grey government.

7

Dr. Dayton Astoria squinted at the display again. His microscope was connected to an overly large monitor in his lab. He only dared to bring up the display when all the students had left the building, the entire faculty had retired for the evening, and his door was locked from the inside so not even Security could access his lab. In some small thought process, he hoped that staring at the problem would simply make it go away. It did not. There in the core he himself had pulled from the deep Antarctic rock was the core sample that contained the proof.

The proof. The truth. The *evidence*. He had called it many things in the last few weeks. None of the terms encompassed the stark reality of the finding. Humans had looped. There was no other way to categorize it. There was no other way to define it. *Humans*, he thought to himself, *had been to the pinnacle before*. And then they had all but disappeared.

Dr. Dayton Astoria of Central Washington University, located in the small college town of Ellensburg, Washington, was for all intents and purposes, currently the most powerful man on the planet. He most assuredly did not want to be.

All of the findings by all the archeologists and anthropologists were not the beginnings of humankind. Leakey at Olduvai Gorge had not found the earliest hominoids on their path to today. Leakey found the malnourished and starving survivors of the first great human race. From those very meager remnants sprang today's society. *We had come and gone, almost.*

He smiled and then loudly guffawed at the universe and all the anthropologists that ever looked for the "missing link." There was never one to find, which explained why after hundreds of years and thousands of expeditions, that since it had never existed, it was therefore never going to be "discovered."

Astoria looked at the display and remembered back to the day it came to the light of a new day. But it was not the first time this sample had seen the light of day. No, of that he was certain.

## 8

The wind had been buffeting and biting at them all day. Temperatures even in summer rarely got above freezing except for a few brief moments on an occasional day. Howling winds could sneak up on the camp without any warning at all.

The supportive guy wires were not their friends. Someone simply had not done their homework when designing the tent system and the supports for the auxiliary structures. When the wind got above fifteen kilometers an hour, the guy wires would start chattering.

At first they would listen to them and try and make out words and songs. During meals and meetings, games were invented to see who could come up with the closest tune the wires might be emulating. At higher velocities the wires began to howl, and at even higher velocities they shrieked. In a matter of days what was an odd way of passing the time became irritating and disturbed everyone's sleep.

The team doctor mentioned to Astoria just two days ago that his supply of muscle relaxers, pain medications, and sleep aids was getting down to the critical level. Astoria noted that his supply of Scotch whiskey was also getting low. He and the doctor laughed and promised to track down the designer of the wire supports and beat the crap out of him or her as a form of therapy when they got stateside again.

Madison, one of the student-interns, did not show up to help run the drill one day. They waited; no one was ever in a hurry when it was this cold. "Haste does not make waste," Astoria, the team leader said, "haste simply makes dead." An hour went by, and one of the college interns suited up and fought the wind over to where Madison's sleeping quarters were.

She came running back across the frozen ground with a note that said, "Can't stand the screaming anymore." Her eyes darted to each of the team. "I looked everywhere; he is not in any of the buildings." They all suited up and found Madison naked face down in a cleft of ice and snow. Already he had frozen solid. Madison had made it two hundred yards, barefoot, sometime during the night. The last dozen yards of his trail were easy to follow; his feet had cracked open and bled.

As the team leader, Astoria took a shovel and covered him over with ice and snow. There was nothing else they could do, clouds were ripping over the low hills, and the screaming wires could be heard plainly above the wind. He told everyone to go back to their bunks, or the dining hall, or the labs to chat, hold hands, pray, or cry. He was unsure what was the norm, never having been faced with death so close, or so personally.

Astoria, accompanied by Everett Pierce, went back to the drill rig and resumed where they had left off. At four hundred feet the drill began to buck and whine, acting as if it had hit something very hard. Rather than damage the expensive coring bit, Astoria began to pull the whole assembly up to investigate. It was easier, as the massive Pierce was helping him with the work. A laborious process under the best of terms, it could take hours of pulling the core samples up from hundreds of feet down. Already they had found fossils, some interesting mineral deposits, and the occasional band of sand. All of these were well within the expected findings.

It was no easy a task even in pleasant surroundings. The wind flapping the tent, the Coleman lantern swinging on its hook, and the thought of dead Madison lying frozen solid a few steps distant weighed heavily on them. As the wind moderated from time to time, it sounded like a human moaning, in pain.

Pierce gasped as one of the pipe couplings spun in his hand, tearing through the glove and laying his palm open. He flung the glove off into a corner of the tent, a trail of red droplets arced through the air.

"God damn it!" Pierce shouted. "Well, son of a bitch!!" He showed Astoria the blood welling from between his clinched fingers.

Astoria shook his head, "That's it for you this trip. Go get the Doc to tend to that. It's going to need some stitches or something. I can finish up here."

Pierce looked around the enclosure and nodded to the affirmative. "Sorry, Dayton, I knew this meant a lot to you. I guess I got distracted about, well, about, you know, Madison and all." Astoria tried to manage a smile and offer some conciliatory remarks, but the wind made the wires scream like a demon. Pierce grimaced from the auditory assault and made a drinking motion with his good hand. Astoria's smile deepened a little and he nodded his head.

He helped Pierce tie a series of fairly clean rags around his hand and patted him on his shoulder as he went into the first of the two doors of the air lock leading to outside.

With Pierce gone he used all of his remaining strength to pull the last few feet of drill pipe from the hole. Part of the last sample slid from the core drill and fell to the plywood floor. It split open as one would imagine a hard-boiled egg breaking after a fall. The wind made the lan-

18

tern swing around. Astoria knelt on one knee to pick up the broken sample.

The shiny metal bit caught his eye. At first he thought it was some contamination from the drilling operation; metal filings were a constant problem. He brushed the sample with his gloved hand.

Odd, the contamination appeared to have stuck itself inside the sample. Biting on his glove he pulled it off and picked at the sample with his fingernail. The metallic part went all the way through the sample. Sagging to both knees, it dawned on him that the core drill had *cut through* this metal. Cutting swirls were evident on both sides of the metal sample.

Astoria smiled; obviously a practical joke had been played on him. One of his interns had dropped the piece on the floor for him to find. No matter. Astoria took the core drill and placed it on top of the collection table and using the hydraulic press forced the remainder of the sample from the bit. It was wedged in more tightly than the other samples. Finally, the drill bit gave up its prize, and he placed the valuable bit in the rack next to the table.

He stopped, frozen to the floor. The sample lying in the special 'v' shaped tray revealed multiple shiny metal parts that had been cut out of the earth hundreds of feet down. This was not a prank, he had been there when the bit went down the hole, and he was there when the bit came back up. What lay before him was a *truth*.

Quickly he broke open the core sample above the metal contamination. Nothing untoward was found. Grabbing sample bags, he placed the mysterious collection in them. These he marked as having been found weeks earlier at a different drill site and at a different depth. Using a code

19

of his mother's birthday and her maiden name, he further labeled the bags.

A colleague of his had announced a new finding of a prehistoric bivalve several years ago. It made a small footnote in some of the scientific journals and was suggested as an important discovery, until some snot-nosed undergrad found that it was not a new discovery; it was simply a forgotten old discovery.

What little fanfare was generated at the first announcement was nothing compared to the ridicule and derision focused on his friend when the error was made public. He went from being a fast-tracked, tenured professor at a Big Ten university to an associate-part-time faculty at a community college near El Paso. Astoria was not going to fail that miserably.

He would take his precious samples back to his full lab in Ellensburg, Washington, at Central Washington State University, for a detailed study before talking to anyone.

9

Ruby La Push had been a star athlete at North Thurston High School in Lacey, Washington. She played soccer in the fall, basketball in the winter, and baseball in the spring and all summer long. Her grades were exceptional. Numerous recruiters called upon her, offering full-ride scholarships and even entry into the farm teams of several organizations.

She finally accepted a basketball scholarship at Pacific Lutheran University. The Seattle Storm sent Loren Jackson to talk to her about basketball after college. Things were going very well that first year at PLU. She got along well with her teammates, and her classes were very interesting.

It started simply as an annoying sore throat. Five days later Ruby La Push was partially paralyzed from the waist down. After the tears and tests and endless therapy, Ruby could manage to take care of herself in a specially modified apartment while using handrails and a cane. Such was the damage caused by the rapid onset of meningitis.

Ruby spent a few weeks after her outplacement from the hospital doing odd jobs on campus. She tried to do some athletic training for the team; however, her limitations due to the braces and canes made it difficult to not re-injure herself, but worse yet, stumble and hurt one of her teammates. After slipping on the slick locker room floor and knocking herself partially senseless, the team coach motioned her into her office later that day.

In her heart she knew this was going to be a good-bye speech of some kind. The locker room was usually filled with high-spirted conversations, laughter, and the bold comments from young women that were at their peak of beauty and desirability. For the moment backs were turned to her as she made her way carefully between the young, sculpted bodies. A few hands reached out and provided a comforting pat on the arm or shoulder.

She stood at the coach's door and waited. Usually a curse was issued first and then the invitation to enter, but this time the coach was waiting, and she opened the door for Ruby and gently pushed her toward a chair, the only chair in the room, sitting across from the coach's. "Please, Ruby, have a seat. I think we both know where we are headed here."

Ruby adjusted her braces and lowered herself into the

chair. "With all this hardware I have, it might have been easier to have just been stood against a wall for the firing squad." She tried to smile at the coach. The coach sat at her desk and stared intently at the worn surface. Not too many years ago she would have lit a cigarette in this very room and added another dark char groove to the edge of the desk.

"I am sorry you feel that way, Ruby." The coach looked up and realized that Ruby was laughing. "Oh, you were always one step ahead of me. I am sorry." She took out a sheaf of papers that were emblazoned with stamps and seals of things legal and from the university.

Ruby smiled, "And all this time I thought a simple, 'G-T-F-O' would have been all it took."

The coach hefted the paperwork and said, "Did you think pulling back two years of a four-year scholarship would not entail a stack of papers to protect the university?" The papers thumped down on the desk, and the coach continued, "In the end I guess it means the same thing, with a simple abbreviation or twenty-five pages of legal mumbo jumbo. More on the mumbo and less on the." Her voice trailed off. "I am so sorry, Ruby, really."

The younger woman nodded politely. In her heart weeks ago she knew this was the most likely course of events. In her head she calculated public relations, news releases, harsh comments from merciless sports reporters chastising the university for not making a place for Ruby to fit in. Still there had to be a place for her to fit in, yet by her own standards no such place existed.

Quietly Ruby went back through her case worker to the university's legal department and made it clear there would not be an acceptable reduced roll simply for the face of the university. She would take advantage of what was available and then slip away. She would reinvent herself as best as she could.

Oddly the university's legal department read her notes more than once and then offered Ruby a job of working with outside law enforcement. This was to help stem the tide of valuable university property being carted off site and sold, sometimes to organizations that may have had at least a passing acquaintance with terrorist organizations.

## 10

Bey began marshaling the forces within Smith, LLC, to do the government's bidding, or whoever-was-paying's bidding. One of his first calls was to Ravenna Lakota. In the peculiar circuitous language of the agents, vague pleasantries were exchanged and a series of random comments were made about the weather, the Seattle Mariners, and next year's crop of grapes grown in Southeast Washington.

To anyone listening, nothing was said that would imply anything. If the listeners had extremely sophisticated equipment, they may have been able to hear birds chirping in the background of Bey's call. They may have also been able to hear a muted radio playing 1970s era rock-and-roll. Ravenna had such sophisticated equipment in her office. In moments she had scrubbed Bey's somewhat mindless chattering about the Mariners. As an imperious Boston fan she could do without his failed attempts to talk sports.

She grinned; Ione had mentioned long ago that Bey's view of professional sports was limited to what he overheard from his brothers-in-law. Ione whispered that she doubted that Neah knew the difference between a free throw, a forced out, and a safety.

Yet, Ravenna frowned, she had seen Bey get shot, stabbed, run over, and even bitten and still continue shooting and killing the bad guys. Ravenna traced a scar down her right forearm where she was injured when the Bey's house blew up one afternoon. She further refined the audio signal to just the bird chirps and the radio broadcast. The bird chirps and the radio signal were both exactly fourteen point five seconds long. Using her sound equipment, she laid one recording over the other.

From the speaker came Neah's voice. "Hey, Babe, please search for Dr. Dayton Astoria, Central Washington University, Ellensburg, Washington. Estimated age thirty-five years." She listened to the recording three times. Using patch cords, she took the recording and fed it into her larger computer.

Neah was what one might call a bit stuffy, so the expression "Hey, Babe" was a little out of character for him. The machine broke the "Hey, Babe" apart into many little fragments that began reassembling themselves on a larger monitor. A picture of Dr. Dayton Astoria emerged.

## 11

In a few weeks, Ruby La Push was the "king pin" of the Central Pierce County High Value Task Force. She stayed up late and rose early, worked nights and weekends. She began to exploit one of the first cross-referencing systems used in pawn shops to record their transactions. Only a few of the more upstanding shops utilized the program. Ruby ignored these after a few weeks. There may have been something to go on, but with her limited time and IT hardware, it would be very difficult. Ruby began focusing on the few pawn shops that refused to latch onto the system. She had a friend drive her to all of them, and there she took pictures of the cable and phone connections.

After months of doing her own research, she became very frustrated. Ruby had exhausted all her own impressive skills and that of her friends in law enforcement. During a very intensive therapy session for her legs, an electronic device used to stimulate nerve endings failed. "God damn technology!" she shouted. A fellow patient using a walker came over. Without saying a word, he took the remote control.

In a moment he disassembled the battery compartment, studied the battery and the connection. Using nothing more than an old pencil taken from a desk, he cleaned the battery ends and the device connection and re-stretched the spring connection. Smiling he handed the device back, "Sometimes 'old school' is the best school."

Ruby took the device and clicked it, which restarted useful operations, and resumed her torturous workout. She smiled back and said "Thanks" for the help. On her way out of the physical therapy facility she scanned the name of her rescuer on the sign-in sheet. Colton Yarrow had written his name in perfect cursive.

They began to develop a friendship. Each one expressed a considerable interest in the other's work. While they occasionally met at therapy sessions and from time to time for a weekend cup of coffee, a greater relationship began to appear on the horizon.

Ruby investigated the limitations of the law and current technology. By happenstance alone, her quarry and friend, Colton Yarrow, was one of the leading experts on capturing miniscule energy signatures, from distant stars to the depths of the oceans. He was also somewhat secretive about his work.

She prepared an exquisite Italian dinner at her apartment and laid her traps. Colton Yarrow was led to his demise with no mercy whatsoever. The rich pasta sauce wafted its miasma through the one-bedroom unit. He greeted Ruby at her front door with a clumsy shake of the hand. From there his nose led him into the kitchen where whatever barriers and boundaries existed were quickly torn down. The rich meat sauce with giant meatballs bubbling away was one attack; the aroma of the cream cheese with roasted garlic slathered on slightly broiled French bread ate into his memory banks. He opened the fridge and saw two six packs of Stella Artois nicely arranged around a true custard Boston cream pie. Whatever defenses the young and handsome Colton Yarrow had arrived with were now being sliced, diced, simmered, and chilled with ruthless precision.

Ruby smiled internally. It was an easy thing to do, somewhat unscrupulous, but needed anyway. Colton Yarrow had undergone a few sessions of psychiatric consoling when he learned that his mother, father, and only sister expired in an automobile accident while Yarrow was but a freshman. Ruby cracked the school's encryption and read the entire file, gleaning from it various things of interest to her. It was a little harder cracking the electronic files of Yarrow's psychiatrist. From that she learned many interesting details, including food that his mother prepared that he sorely missed. In the end, in spite of Yarrow's being sometimes wheelchair bound, Yarrow and Ruby enjoyed an active romance; it just took a little more imagination.

Yarrow studied the pictures that Ruby had taken and was at first very put off that his doctoral thesis in some part was going to be purloined into something very much different. Ruby shook her head sadly from side to side. "Well, I was so sure that this would be a slam dunk for you!"

Colton Yarrow was stuck into his chair with little possibility of escape, Ruby's stunning figure pointedly counterbalanced by four chilling Stella Artois in a bucket of ice in one hand and a large platter of homemade chips and a huge mountain of guacamole in the other.

Yarrow mumbled, "God damn you, woman! I knew you were the personification of the lady devil; I just knew it!" He shook his head from side to side and top to bottom. "Well, I will help you out this once."

Ruby had been waiting. She stepped aside, and there lay a platter of huge chicken, beef, and pork ravioli, the monster ones that Yarrow's mother used to make, the ones where three of them were a full meal. "God damn you, again! You are a temptress of low standards! One of the worst! Clearly no shame whatsoever!"

Yarrow could only mutter. Sitting in his lap, Ruby poured an Artois into a frosted glass. There was no surrender, merely conquest.

## 12

Bey began shuffling through web pages of technical writings. The Smiths sent him text books. The books had been gleaned from college book stores, various used book sellers, and in several cases simply stolen from public libraries. These had been gone through with a meticulous eye: any reference to Dr. Dayton Astoria had been highlighted, any of his research was tabbed, noted, cut out, or somehow identified so that Bey did not have to do the digging himself.

Neah kissed Ione good bye in the morning and drove the pickup truck to Portland, Oregon, about an hour and a half away. The pickup truck was a custom hot rod built for Bey by a brother-in-law in Tenino, Washington. While plain and unpretentious, it was built on a Corvette frame. When Bey asked how many horsepower were under the hood, the brother-in-law smiled and said, "North of 650, and that is just the twin turbos. You'll be much higher when you kick the nitrous into it." Bey had to smile politely and be grateful, as he had no idea what his brother-in-law was talking about.

In Portland he went to Powell's Books and rummaged through the sections on geology, Antarctica, plate tectonics, and the history of exploration of the frozen land. From there he went to his fictitiously rented mail box and retrieved several envelopes of material. Some were from the Smiths; some were items he himself had ordered.

His last stop was at the Portland Market where he picked up a piece of fused glass jewelry from Rachel, a vendor that Ione favored. It shifted colors in his hand from slight reds to faint blues; he was sure Ione would like it.

On his way north to his house, the custom cellular telephone built into the truck rang. It was voice-activated and totally hands-free.

"Yes?" There was a series of slight clicks. Off to the center of the dashboard, a very small closed-circuit camera scanned the interior of the truck. Bey waited; this was the usual manner in which calls were received. When a small LED blinked on the dashboard, Bey recited a sentence, "Mary had a little lamb, its fleece was white as snow." In moments his voice had been analyzed for stress indicators and the interior of the truck scanned for anyone other than Bey.

"Mr. Bey, we were wondering about the progress you have made on the task at hand." It was a voice devoid of inflection and may have been computer-generated.

Bey gave a soft smile and said, "As always, a daunting task. I have read everything and have been in contact with several fellow..." he paused searching for the right word.

The voice provided guidance, "Friends?"

Bey nodded his head to the affirmative, "Yes, friends, I suppose. Suffice it to say that if the information possessed by Dr. Astoria ever hit the main-stream media, social unrest might result."

There was a pause, and the disconnected voice began, "Social unrest? That would be the politest way of describing the riots, wars, governmental collapse, and mass hysteria on a global scale. Social unrest indeed."

Bey nosed around traffic on the north side of the Interstate 5 Bridge spanning the Columbia River. "Shall I assume that we want the evidence secured and Dr. Astoria's cooperation, hmm, counted upon?" There was a pause.

The voice sounded even more disconnected, even more disembodied. "By whatever means necessary. And we are in receipt of information that others may be in possession of similar materials." There was a click and the call was ended. Bey floored the throttle and enjoyed the power of the huge V-8 as it pushed him back into the seat.

## 13

Colton Yarrow was injured in a motorcycle accident at an early age. For the most part he was confined to a wheelchair. At times he could rise and negotiate a short distance, like from the bed to the bath, or out to the kitchen for a snack, if he used a pair of canes or the walker. Like Ruby, he had more than enough brains to accept his condition and move on. He was fond of Stephen Hawking, and he paraphrased a quote, "Name one place in the universe my mind cannot take me."

Colton was investigating radio frequency issues prevalent everywhere; stars gave it off, planets transmitted it, animals produced it, and everything everywhere was a transmitter, reflector, or receiver of this energy. It was an oft-studied energy, dating back to well before Tesla began experimenting with it.

Colton's area of expertise was in the sensing and reporting of the minuscule amounts of energy given off by computer networks and their associated cabling. In his work he had hand-fabricated a few devices for testing and had surreptitiously installed several of the innocuous items around campus. They worked. His subsequent attack was on the upper tier of protected circuits, which involved local stock brokerages and a handful of banks. He did not gain anything personally from the data; it was merely a test of his equipment.

It was somewhat surprising when one day at his lab two gentlemen walked in, reeking of government service. They asked many questions about Colton's research. And while they asked many questions of Colton's past, it was clear they already knew the answers; it was just box checking, a word dance and nothing more.

In their concluding remarks the gentlemen made it very clear that Colton Yarrow's work was undergoing severe scrutiny at a very high level. Colton could hardly express his mirth, "And just who might be reviewing *my* work at a high level?"

The agents stopped. "Suffice it to say, Mr. Yarrow, while *we* may not fully understand your work, there are those that do." One of the agents tapped the spine of a book authored by S. Lockwood of the venerable firm of Hatfield and Dawson of Seattle, the world's leading authority on the subject. "That can be a very good thing, or a very bad thing." They produced a stack of legal forms, indicating that Mr. Yarrow was now considered a "Security Issue." His attention to the forms should cause him to reflect on the hefty civil as well as criminal penalties should he fail to comply with any one of two-hundred items dutifully listed thereon.

One of the items on the list was particularly onerous to Colton Yarrow: every seventy-two hours he was required to update his work on a remote server. He failed to do so one weekend, thinking that the government was taking Saturday and Sunday off as was he. Monday morning the President of the university met him at the door to the lab.

PLU's president had graduated from the Air Force Academy, retiring after 22 years of active duty as a Lieutenant Colonel. The president made it very clear to Colton Yarrow that compliance with governmental security directives was his first and foremost responsibility, should he wish to continue his work at the university. Colton set his smart watch, his cell phone, and his laptop to sound ever more strident alarms when the check-in time drew near.

## 14

In a cave carved out of a hillside in the southernmost part of the Hindu Kush sat a man sipping strong and bitter tea. The kerosene heater that was poorly vented barely fought back the cold of the mountain of stone.

"That's all right, in a few months it will be so hot and dusty we will pray for winter again." He said this to no one in particular; he sat alone in a hand-carved anteroom of the cave. The smell of kerosene and sweat and stink and humans packed too closely together for far too long assailed his senses again.

He looked at the battery-operated clock that hung off an iron spike driven into the cave wall. *"Ten minutes and a reprieve,"* he thought to himself. In ten minutes the impressive array of United States spy satellites would finally dip below the horizon, and the cave would empty. Dozens of men, women, and even children would dash outside to breathe fresh air, to stretch their legs, to bask in the cold sunlight for exactly twenty-four point seven-five minutes.

A modest safety factor was built into the time to ensure that everyone could make it back into the cave before the next spy-satellite peeked over the horizon from its polar orbit. Buckets of urine and feces were dragged from the cave and poured out onto the ground a hundred meters away. A rusty old fan was set up in the adit to pull the stinking air from the hole in the ground that was home. Tangles of logs would be pulled back from the extreme northern portal of the cave to help wash the air from every part.

It seemed the stink had permeated every pore of the dense stone. The respite from the olfactory onslaught was more illusory than real. Still and all, he enjoyed lighting up a decadent cigarette from the U.S.A. and inhaled deeply from it.

He looked over his shoulder and saw a young man, a teenager actually, dressed much the same way he was in traditional garb. An AK-47 knock-off hung from a rope slung over his shoulder.

The young man stared at his watch intently. He was the timekeeper for the six breaks they could have each twenty-four-hour period. The lessons learned by the death of many friends from drone strikes and cruise missiles made this a new function of their religion, their way of life. Help from many sources kept them apprised of the spy-sat time table.

He and his team paid more attention to rocket launches from the U.S.A. than most Americans did. It might be a fun event for tourism in the Florida area to have rocket launch parties; here on the other side of the world it might mean fewer opportunities to go outside and enjoy clean air. The Americans were always sending up more satellites to improve their look-down capabilities.

And that was not their only concern: two months ago a child acting as shepherd for some goats a few kilometers away was found playing with a solar-powered drone. It had less than a meter-wide wing span and was made from plastic so thin and clear that it would be very difficult to see at more than a few hundred meters. It was electric, and silent. It bore no markings, no serial numbers, no name and date or place of manufacture. He guessed it was hand-crafted by those bastard Americans in the Columbia River Valley east of Portland, Oregon.

A sigh passed from his chest, such technology would be difficult to evade forever, and it was time to return to the repugnant cave that was his home. The time keeper was lightly tapping on a tin tea cup with a metal spoon. One last deep breath of clean cold mountain air, and he entered the cave.

## 15

Ruby La Push had to find some line of work that did not require her legs. Computer studies were an obvious choice. Her relationship with Colton made the most difficult aspects easy to grasp. The university computer network became her playground, and when cracked open, it revealed a universe of other off-campus systems to exploit. While fun, it had no reward, at least tangible, saleable, or marketable.

It was her work with the Pierce County Major Crimes Division in concert with the High Value group that was the most inspirational and challenging. She excelled at digging into a system. Her sheriff friends had her sift data from old cases. Ruby had a knack for finding threads between cases, this stolen property ending up at a pawn shop on the other side of the state, a stolen delivery van of tools and a sudden influx of construction equipment appearing on Craig's list a thousand miles away. A frustrating theme was played out in meeting after meeting; gathering of evidence had to follow rules: specific rules, strangling rules, rules that meant the bad guys walked away with their ill-gotten gains and victimized home and business owners were left with nothing except bills to repair damage and dealing with insurance claims.

Ruby began to feel as frustrated as anyone in the law

enforcement community she interacted with. She set her mind to figure out the theft of university property. The captain she reported to listened intently to the young woman. "Okay, you have done some great work, and now you want to take on the world? For free?" He shook his head, "Well, I have no idea where this goes, but it will go. Give me a few days to call in some favors."

In two weeks Ruby La Push began creating a collecting program for the theft of university property from all over the West Coast. In three weeks she began sorting theft reports and matching those with the sales listings across the globe. In four weeks sixteen students and seven professors were arrested from virtually every school in the Pac-12.

One of the recipients of the money from the stolen equipment was very irritated. It was going to require some additional resources to make up the loss of what was virtually free money. The stag-horned handled knife flipped in the air and was caught in the opposite hand. "Well, like no one has said before, 'make your opponent useful,' for a while."

16

One day when Ruby was alone, a very business-like woman knocked on her door. "Hello, you must be Ruby La Push? May I come in to chat?" The woman, who identified herself as Mrs. T, sat in a chair in the living room and asked many questions of Ruby La Push.

In the end Mrs. T asked, "Well, Ruby, I am sure you have heard all the hearts and flowers speeches. By now you have heard every lie and half-truth about your condition.

Suffice it to say that you will live twenty years less than the average; you will be bothered by infections, falls, false promises, and more; and yet you can still have a purpose, a meaningful purpose. Are you interested?"

At first Ruby was angry, then as she had done before, accepted her condition and decided to move on as best she could. However, she was thunderstruck by the salary and benefits Mrs. T offered. It would not get her legs back, but it would pretty much take care of everything else.

Two days later a moving van picked her and her possessions up, and she was moved to a townhouse in an upscale neighborhood on Mercer Island, just outside of Seattle. She even had a part-time housekeeper-cook at no cost. The next day the computer was installed in the large office off the living room.

Ruby asked why an electric generator was being installed in the garage. The service person said, "With a generator this size, you will be able to power everything in your house. This switch automatically moves from city power to generator power and back." He patted a large unit adjacent to the generator. "And this battery pack is what the power feeds through to your house."

Ruby stared at the unit with its cooling fans and cables. "Why does it do that?"

He shrugged his shoulders, "Whoever is paying this bill does not want you to ever lose power for even a second. Heck, the world could end, and you will still be watching your soaps without interruption." He smiled, handed her the operations manual, picked up his tool box, and left.

Ruby was a little concerned that none of the workers that came to her house to add the handrails, adjust the door swings, install the computer, and now install the backup generator arrived in vehicles with company names on them. They were all brand new grey vans and trucks. No decals, no contractor license information, no phone numbers, no identification at all.

When she mentioned this to Mrs. T with a note of worry in her voice, Mrs. T laughed and said, "Ruby! My goodness! You'd think we were spies or something! Don't worry, we like our privacy, and we thought you would too."

Ruby quickly mastered the computer system. When she had questions, all she had to do was literally push a button and one of the monitors on the wall would spring to life. The monitor would be filled with the image of a very professional-appearing man or woman who would answer all of her questions about the machine, day or night.

Her first assignment was to research any information about a Professor Dayton Astoria from Central Washington University.

When Colton heard of the arrangements, he objected strongly. They were going to make them live too far apart. He confided that he enjoyed their odd relationship and did not want to lose contact with Ruby as the result of a mere employment opportunity.

Ruby countered by showing Colton her one-month's pay that she received in advance and the corresponding deposit slip.

Still, Colton was unhappy, until Ruby commented, "For us, being the way we are, this is just the way it is going to be. Do you want to be married to a poor cripple, or a rich cripple?"

## 17

Ruby La Push turned on her computer at two in the morning and began working. An icon began blinking on one of the overly large monitors. Beneath the icon were the initials "Dr. D. A." She assumed it was a file that had been sent to her from Mrs. T relating to Dr. Dayton Astoria. Ruby was partially right. When the mouse clicked on the icon, her screen filled with small color video pictures. They were images from closed- circuit television cameras.

Some of the images were of what appeared to be inside a modest house or apartment, inside an office filled with books, and more--much more. One of the images shifted back and forth a little. She scrolled the mouse over and clicked on that image. The monitor next to that sprang to life, filled with the image of a man she recognized as Astoria working at a computer while lifting a small free weight in one hand. He would type with one hand then shift the weight to the other hand and exercise his other arm.

Ruby La Push shifted her gaze from image to image and realized that she was watching covert images of another human being. She did not sleep for two days as she followed Dr. Dayton Astoria through his illicitly captured life.

At the end of those two days, Ruby threw her collection of online accounting courses into the recycle bin. This was going to be far more interesting than fussing over equations detailing depreciation on toilets and sewage lift stations in commercial buildings. Far more interesting.

## 18

It was the last week they were going to be on the ice. Astoria cobbled up an excuse to take a snowmobile out for a spin. He told Pierce and the others he wanted to think about things, including Madison.

It had taken Astoria the better part of two days to chip frozen Madison out of the ice and stuff him into a sleeping bag. There had been the sad duty of telling Madison's mother and surviving brother about his death. It was some of the worst twenty minutes Astoria had spent on the ice. The wind howled and made those damn wires scream. The radio telephone reception and undoubtedly the transmission itself were simply awful.

Static bursts from the aurora Australis made the voices sound unearthly. It was all very unnerving, even after Pierce sat down next him and poured Astoria four fingers of very fine Scotch.

Madison's mother did not take the news well and began crying uncontrollably during the transmission. Albion, the brother, hung in there as best he could. Astoria vowed to accompany the body back to the Metaline Falls community north of Spokane for the internment. Astoria gulped the Scotch and thanked Albion for understanding. Astoria hung up the phone in the special cradle and placed both hands over his face.

Tears streamed down under his palms. Pierce put a beefy arm around him and said, "Boss that was a brave thing you did. You said the right things. They were proud to hear that their son and brother took part in a great expedition to further." Pierce's voice faded away, overshadowed by the screaming wires.

"Still Boss-Man, you did better than anyone else could have." He left the bottle on the table and quietly exited the radio shack. He turned the overhead lights off, leaving Astoria illuminated by the sickly green glow of the radios and computers. Astoria wept silently.

## 19

Two days later Astoria had the snow machine packed with a tent, food, water, and extra fuel. He waved good-bye to the team. They would be spending the next few days tearing the camp apart and packing everything up. The team doctor tried to get him to delay his departure, as it was lightly snowing and would be for a few hours more. Astoria politely declined, as it fit his plans to literally cover his tracks.

Astoria refused to allow anyone else to have to handle Madison's remains. Pierce trudged over to help Astoria place Madison in the sled, but he was waved off. He felt it was his obligation to secure the corpse of his associate and no one else's. That was yesterday.

Today he gunned the engine and tore off from the camp, the cold wind slapping him in the face even through the polar shield. His course made him drive west for approximately 45 miles, then directly south toward the tip of the Patriot Mountains. He could see the prominences on the distance horizon of snow. It was near dusk when he arrived, often having to stop and use the GPS device to help guide him.

The rudimentary maps he had hand-copied from the Smithsonian were only marginally useful for navigating.

They came into play when he neared an outcropping of rock. It was not what the drawings and maps depicted at all. Yet, there was the cleft in the mountain, the noteworthy cracked twin peak of dark mountain stone to the east, and the narrow valley pointing almost directly at the South Pole. He had to be in the right spot. Yet the outcropping in question was missing, the area a field of broken stone.

Dismounting, he examined the stone. It was shattered into chunks. Nothing on the icy continent could have created that pattern of destruction. Using his climbing gear, he began a risky ascent in the twilight. He got to a slight convex area of the face and sat down. It was beautiful, the setting sun angry red on the distant horizon, and the Aurora Australis shimmering overhead. He took in the sights for a moment and then turned his head lamp on and picked his way across the promontory.

He missed the remains of the first three holes, but found the fourth, fifth, and then the rest. It was obvious that someone had drilled holes into the rock face and placed explosives in them. Tucked under a rock was a bit of burned-out fuse line. He carefully wrapped it in a handkerchief and placed that in his pocket.

Whatever Shackleton, Falcon, and others had found had been purposefully covered up by a sizeable explosion. Astoria then carefully picked his way back to the snow machine and made a hurried camp.

20

On her last day working for the university, Colton Yarrow wheeled up to Ruby's desk in the Admin Building.

She set the phone down and smiled. "Hey, how is our project going?"

Yarrow remained silent, and with a straight face he handed Ruby a flash drive.

"Oh? What might this be?" she turned the drive over and over in her fingers. Yarrow remained implacable.

"Well, aren't we being dramatic? Okay, let me plug this in." Ruby began to insert the drive and stopped, "This isn't a 'get even' moment because of the Italian dinner is it? I'm not going to crash the system with a virus am I?"

He merely raised an eyebrow in response.

The drive slid into the port. Ruby's screen went blank and then fluttered through the spectrum of visible light. She nervously sought a reaction from Yarrow; there was none.

A spread sheet began forming in the fog of colors. It grew until it filled all three of Ruby's screens. Stunned, she watched the details scroll down, and down, hundreds of lines of entries, thousands of data points were revealed. Ruby sat back in her chair, "How did you do this?"

Finally, Yarrow smiled and with some effort reached down to the space between the desks. He pulled on the computer cabling.

"So? That is a computer cable that connects the desktop to the network and then the web." Ruby followed the cord up and down its length. Connections, cable, more connections, nothing remarkable.

Still silent Yarrow raised the desk lamp and turned it over revealing a scant collection of electronics. He nodded toward the screens and finally spoke, "Look closely."

The data had continued to scroll, now revealing tens of thousands of lines, hundreds of thousands of, possibly millions of data points. Ruby tapped the scroll arrows and slowed the data stream. She stopped on a single line. It was time stamped for 18:37:42 last evening. She advanced a single line, it was time stamped 18:37:43. Ruby moved the cursor to the right and found a description of the event. The screen revealed that at 18:37:43 Ruby La Push entered a command on her desk top, in effect locking it for the evening.

Turning to Yarrow she said, "Impressive."

Yarrow smiled, and said "Go to line forty-four-thousand-nineteen."

Ruby did as directed. "How?" Shown in the data was the laptop Ruby employed at home being used to surf the web. Yarrow produced his cellphone and brought up the exterior cabling for her apartment. The picture was a little fuzzy, but a close-up of enough detail to reveal the tattle-tale he had installed.

"How long have you been spying on me?" A frown flashed across her face.

Colton Yarrow reached into his back pack and produced a nicely wrapped gift, with a tag stating "For Ruby."

"For me? How sweet!" Ruby began tearing into the package with gusto. Yarrow rolled his wheelchair back a good three feet. Several of the Campus Security Team and members of the Sheriff's office turned to watch the unwrapping.

A smile crept across Colton Yarrow's face; he began recording the event with his cellphone. Ruby set the package down, having run into multiple layers of heavy packaging tape. From her desk she extracted a pair of scissors. "Making this difficult are we?" With one snip of the scissors the top of the package shot upwards. Ruby sat back in fright.

In the small burst of compressed air, a single column of thin plastic rose from the package, dragging into full view the skimpiest of nighttime lingerie. It appeared to be manufactured of nearly transparent gauze in a red color. The office exploded into hysterical laughter; numerous cellphone cameras were instantly deployed. Ruby shrieked in profound embarrassment.

"I do believe that is the article you were looking at last Thursday evening at 21:55 hours on the Victoria's Secret web site? Or was it this one from Frederick's of Hollywood?" He would have been able to pull the second package out of his back pack; however, he was precluded from completing this mission as Ruby clubbed him upside the head with one of her canes. Colton Yarrow had failed to accurately calculate the range of an angry woman with a cane.

One of the Security Officers whispered a line from *South Park*, "Cool, cripple fight!"

21

Kadar was privileged in many ways. Handsome, tall, he looked more Navajo than Afghani. His parents were rich from their affiliation with the Shah of Iran, but then, as they always seemed to do, it fell apart. Kadar was enrolled at the University of Michigan, partially owing to the Business School and partially owing to his relatives that lived nearby. It gave him a sense of family the first year and then a life-line thereafter.

When the Shah fell, his family was routed and sent packing across the border into Afghanistan. They hid their money and slowly worked themselves across Europe to

Montreal and then into the Chicago area. They immersed themselves into American society and faded from view.

Not Kadar. He despised the opulence that the Shah displayed, fancy ornate uniforms, immaculate hair, private jets; nothing like what Kadar felt his people should be like. He studied hard and excelled in many areas. However, he felt detached, removed, and separate from the rest of the student body. Kadar only felt at ease when at Middle Eastern events or at friends' homes. Here they read and talked politics, yet he felt isolated from most, if not all of his associates who were deeply involved in Islam. His desires and their faith seemed to be separate, to be on different paths and on different levels. Kadar began to see Islam as nothing more than a resource to be exploited.

Nine-eleven was now over by two-plus decades; the deceased bin Laden had been tossed off a U.S. warship in an unceremonious manner. Kadar worked at an advertising agency that specialized in serving the Middle Eastern Community in the Rust Belt.

He realized that unless you had a plan going forward, snatching a random headline only moved you to the head of the list for a drone strike or something more slow and painful at the hands of operatives of the United States. He wanted to be rich, famous, powerful, and no singular effort would provide those things. Kadar and his associates used private chat rooms and exploited the internet to build a network, a network that the United States intelligence community feared most; they were unaffiliated, self-financed, and under every radar.

One of the members was an intern at the Smithsonian, and she had a very interesting story to tell about another former intern: a Doctor Dayton Astoria.

## 22

Budd Todd bore the name of his great-great grandfather who was an early pioneer in the Pacific Northwest. He had served his country with distinction in both Afghanistan and Iraq. After being treated for a mild case of post-traumatic stress disorder, he continued his service as an electronic warfare specialist. Even though he wore no uniform, he was still a captain in the United States Marine Corps.

Today, he wore the loudest Hawaiian shirt he could find, attempting to outdo his colonel. He failed. The colonel wore what one might consider the most flaming gay neon pink and green shirt that had Elvis on one side and Mickey Mouse on the other. Budd Todd took out a crisp five and put it in the team's party box. He sneered at the colonel, and the colonel gave him the finger back. Such was the typical Friday in the "Tube" as they called it.

The Tube was built under part of Denver International Airport, somewhat supporting popular myth and legend that the government was communicating with alien life forms. They were not. They were using a variety of technologies beyond compare to scan places for people and things that might be a threat.

Budd Todd was assigned to a group whose task was to scour remote places for hidden people. Their mission was to discover those people and pass on the information. He was quite skilled. A pen and a small note sat in a plastic box on his desk. The paper bore the finely imprinted picture of the White House along with a brief handwritten note that said, "Thanks, we owe you." with the initials of the

President of the United States. Below that was the number three crossed out.

Budd Todd, using the elaborate tools of his trade, found the number three bad guy in the world. A contract kill team eradicated another person that was a threat to the United States.

Budd sighed; today there was a new number three. There would always be yet another bad guy that needed attention.

While the media frolicked over the public side of the enemies list and made great headlines of when a bad guy fell, they were wrong. The government had many lists of threats; mostly no one outside of the Tube knew who they were. Budd thought he remembered something from Shakespeare that the real threat lies with those behind the throne.

Tomorrow the new spy-sat was going to be hurled into space; this gave Budd the opportunity to play. Without using too much precious fuel, Budd could advance or retard the orbits of his collection of space birds. And thus he could sometimes find people who knew the satellite schedule as well as he. He had been peering down in Iraq and Afghanistan for some time, which gave him mental pictures of the terrain and the general activities in a handful of areas. On his off hours, Budd would continue to search the web for information on interesting topography and geology that might harbor unfriendly people.

23

The Trade Group liaison read the reports from her mentor who was now employed by the Smiths. Things were in motion that Business did not want in motion. She already knew that information had been bought and sold across the internet. Rumors did not have to be bound to fact to be destructive. Yet, here was a fact that spawned rumor.

Fortunately, the facts were only held by a few, and those were under close scrutiny. She called up the picture of Dr. Astoria on her tablet. "A book worm brings about the end of the world," she muttered into the air of her office. Still, if Astoria and his collection of tidbits could be secured in a timely manner, he might live to continue his work on the ice. If not, then an unmarked grave or a very deep spot in the ocean might be his reward.

She brushed an errant bit of hair from her face and scanned her other reports. The Shackleton data was old enough to almost be irrelevant. Those peculiar remarks could easily be dealt with as those of malnourished and nearly frozen humans at the outer edge of survival. Still, Shackleton left no stone unturned and was not only a consummate leader but also highly intelligent. His family saying was *"Fortitudine vincimus,"* which she thought meant 'By Endurance, we prevail" or something like that.

Whatever Shackleton found and brought back to Great Britain weighed heavily upon him. There were numerous business failures, he was heavily in debt, and toward the end, drank champagne in the morning, ostensibly to deaden the pain of a failing heart. He succumbed to a presumed heart attack and was buried on an island on his last expedition.

Falcon Scott collected during the fatal Discovery Expedition more data and evidence; the Ketchum Expedition had recovered those artifacts and carefully removed the implicating pages of the diaries. The rest were small snippets of this and that, ruthlessly hunted down. Or so they

48

thought. Houses of heirs were burgled. Safety deposit boxes unsealed and contents removed. Business had many such skills to employ. Still after all these years, persistent rumors came and went; each one a threat to Business and the continuity thereof.

Her part of the puzzle was to secure for Business a bright future. Anything less than supporting the economy was flawed thinking. Sometimes a few sacred aboriginal graves had to be relocated in the dark of night; but only if the refinery, overpass, weapons depot, or power plant were good for Business.

Sometimes endangered species would get just a little more endangered if the shopping mall, port facility, or rail yard was really important. She smirked upon recalling how Business gave hundreds of sling shots anonymously to delinquent little brats. That effort most thoroughly solved the nesting problems of a lesser species of feathered rat that was delaying a cruise ship terminal, but only because it was good for Business.

Most people simply did not have the intelligence to grasp the fundamental nature of how important Business was for the good of everyone. She sipped her latte. "Yes," she whispered, "And sometimes a few of them have to die, but only if it is really important for Business."

Her mentor at the Smiths' chided her once, "Business is good for everybody, and sometimes, a few bodies are good for Business." She smiled. Her computer chirped. A message flashed across the screen. Dr. Astoria was not the only one with physical evidence, it seemed. She frowned deeply, "Damn it." In her heart she knew that Astoria had only parts of what the Ketchum Expedition had brought back, and now others, possibly more.

## 24

Adiba helped Astoria at the Smithsonian from time to time. The museums and their storerooms, warehouses, and basements covered blocks and blocks, and that was the main complex in Washington, D.C. The storage facilities on the outskirts were something of legend. Rumors abounded about what lay catalogued away. She heard the stories of FOIA requests to search for the Ark of the Covenant after the first Indiana Jones movie hit the screen.

While the world knew that FOIA meant "Freedom of Information Act," it was locally known as the "Fools of Intellectual Absence." One staffer was complimented on the rapidity with which his FOIA requests disappeared from his desk. Sadly, the closed-circuit television unit showed him shredding stacks of documents on his coffee breaks.

Time and again some delusional person would try to break in to find alien artifacts, President Kennedy's head, or the 500-mile-per-gallon carburetor. For a time Adiba was assigned the task of writing notes and answering multitudes of emails about everything the Smithsonian did *not* have stored away. After a while she stopped caring about what someone's sister heard about this, that, and everything else that was part of a conspiracy theory.

She learned to hate public radio interviews with every nut job that was allowed air time. The further from the truth the interview went, the greater the number of calls and emails. One of the stranger tasks she had was to open packages and attempt to identify the contents.

Her friend, Security Officer Copalis, had the onerous

duty to run the questionable packages through x-ray machines and explosive detectors. She would swing by his small office in front of the building and stare at the stack of packages.

"Oh, my, what's the haul today?" Adiba asked one morning.

Copalis looked up from his desk and pointed at a pile and said "Desiccated chipmunk, desiccated raccoon, desiccated dog, shark in olive oil, four boxes of cow bones, and a mystery pile of stuff that you should just throw out."

She stared at one box that was damp on the outside. "Err, what is that one?"

Copalis read a tag, "Oh, yeah, shark in olive oil."

Adiba looked skeptical, "So, why olive oil?"

Copalis read the packing list, "Says here that Mr. and Mrs. Warden while on a walk along the beach at Seaside, Oregon, discovered what they thought was an alien life form."

She frowned and stepped back, thinking she could smell something rotting inside the box, "Okay, still does not answer the olive oil. What does that do for it?"

Copalis had been waiting patiently. He reached into the top drawer of his desk and withdrew a large piece of fish and wolfed it down.

"Makes it slide down real good. Wanna bite?" He offered another piece of fish to Adiba.

Adiba stepped further back and with horror on her face said, "No, no you did not just eat a piece of that did you?"

Copalis wiped his lips with a napkin and brought out the whole container of fish and chips, the Friday fare at the cafeteria. "Sure, why not, it's Friday, and I'm a good Catholic."

They both laughed. "Okay, anything else I need to know?" Adiba inquired.

Copalis waved his hand, "Nay, nay, I say. I will throw this stuff on the cart and haul it down for you on the freight elevator. Why don't you grab a chair and enjoy the sun for a moment while I do that?"

Adiba settled in the chair and looked skyward toward the sunlight streaming in through the glass roof. "Thanks! I will." One small envelope had a mysterious message in it about artifacts the Smithsonian had. She scanned and sent the message to Kadar.

## 25

Tex sat back in the chair. "Okay, I can do that."

Ms. Smith smiled her lopsided smile.

"Report back when completed." She ran her fingers over the glass plate that made up the top of her desk. "And, thanks."

He rose, tipped his head forward a little and turned toward the door.

"Tex?" Ms. Smith asked.

He stopped and turned back to face the seated woman. "Yes?"

"How are you doing?" She folded her hands together on the glass plate.

"I'm doing okay. Some days are better than others." He tried to force a small smile on his rugged face.

"You have been through a lot; do you need some time off?" She asked, her brow knitting together.

Tex looked at the floor and then around the room, finally resting his gaze on Ms. Smith's face. "I appreciate your concern, but being at work takes my mind off of other things." His gaze again circled the room, "Well, it sort of helps anyway."

"Tex, you are the rock we anchor to around here. On the other hand, with that in mind, you take whatever time you need." She looked down at the desk again. "What the priest said at the services were, well, they were very fitting." Looking up at Tex she tried to smile again, but it came across her face as a frown. "I am not the only one here that misses Nemah."

Tex was going to say something in response, but all he managed was a nod of his head; it was still too soon, and hurt too much.

## 26

In the morning Dr. Astoria broke camp and carefully packed everything back on the machine. He took out his laptop and hooked the satellite phone into it. When things were linked up and running he called up one of the LOES, Low Earth Orbit Satellites, which displayed real time weather for the Southern Hemisphere. His fingers were smarting from the cold, so he typed for a bit and then placed his mittens back on until the pain subsided.

He got the image he was looking for, a massive storm was roaring across the Ross Ice Shelf and was pointed like a thousand-kilometer-wide sledgehammer at him. This is what he had hoped for. The timing of his ride was directly related to the few and far between satellites that crossed this section of the earth.

If he timed it just right, the snow would obscure any tracks of this passage in mere minutes. If he timed it just wrong, he would break through a hidden crevasse and plummet to his death potentially hundreds of feet beneath the surface. He twisted the throttle of the snow machine to wide open; it was now a race that would be decided by things he could not control.

It was with great relief that he heard Pierce on the radio.

"Boss-Man, I hope that is you coming toward us. You have a whiteout not more than two klicks behind you." Pierce had climbed to the top of the ridge that sheltered most of the camp from the direct onslaught of the prevailing winds.

"Right, buddy, did you bake a cake?" Astoria asked.

Pierce smiled, "Nah, well, yes, but we figured you were watching your weight, so we ate it yesterday. Sorry." Astoria laughed into the radio and looked over his shoulder. Ice streams as sharp as glass began tickling the fiberglass of the snow machine. He raced the grasp of a frozen devil that last five kilometers into camp.

## 27

Budd found a spot that just didn't make any sense. There was an area that appeared to be the bottom of a small gully that was consistently several tens of degrees warmer than the surrounding area. He checked sources from other airborne assets, read up on the local region, and nothing gave any reason for this to be happening.

Today he swung a spy-sat around to look down into the area of this gully when the local temperature would be at its lowest. Around 03:00 hours local time, the Condor spy satellite, as he called it, would be fairly low on the horizon well to the east of the gully; this would give Budd Todd his glimpse that he was looking for.

## 28

Those devilish Americans had yet again shifted the orbit of one of their damnable satellites. It was only by a miracle that someone who was watching for the launch of yet another satellite noticed that an existing one had sped up ever so slightly.

The radio crackled on the chest of the young man with the tea cup and spoon. Instantly he began shouting and banging on the cup. Everyone outside who was enjoying the cold mountain air very early in the morning crushed out their cigarettes, threw the last gulps of tea on the ground, and ran toward the cave entrance. Hurriedly the fan was dragged back in. When the cover was secured, all the residents breathed in the stale and fetid cave air and looked longingly at the wood and cloth cover.

Akil walked back to his bench and laptop, saddened by the fact that his breaks of fresh air were most likely cut by a least one third from this point going forward.

## 29

Condor began taking pictures and high resolution video from hundreds of miles in the heavens. Several methods were used to peer over a foreground mountain top and into the distant valley. Budd Todd stared quizzically at the raw data.

## 30

Akil Tamur again took up his place on his makeshift chair and skillfully pecked at the laptop. His first name meant intelligent, thoughtful, or one who reasons, depending upon the mood of his surviving family members. His last name had many different meanings, such as lion's den or lair, or even secretary to a king; the true meaning of it died with his parents.

The Soviet invaders periodically rained mortar fire onto suspected mujahedeen locations. Often the Soviets were so totally inebriated they misread coordinates or just fired at something they imagined. His family was awakened when the first blasts erupted at the north end of their tiny village. From too numerous encounters they knew the attack plan: pound the village from one direction and drive the suspected combatants into a kill zone already set up.

Akil's father grabbed his two sons and began running ninety degrees to the axis of the town. In this manner he hoped to run to safety away from the death falling from the heavens and avoid the machine guns that were already lighting up the south end of the village with angry tongues of tracer fire.

Akil was under one of his father's arms looking backwards toward the village; his mother had grabbed some pictures and family mementos, which made her forty yards slower. Akil heard the whistle of the shell and then watched the very earth beneath his mother vaporize into a fire ball. The concussion threw Akil's father forward, losing the grip on his sons.

Akil was crushed under the weight of his father coming down on him. He gasped for air. Talib, his brother, cried out. The next blast was so very close that Akil was lifted from the ground along with his father and thrown five yards down the path. Shells pounded the village into flaming rubble. Those few that survived the mortars and ran south were cut down by the machine guns.

When Akil awoke, his father was dead, brutally eviscerated by the shell fragments. The upper half of Talib stared toward the sky with partially opened eyes. Akil watched as the huge Soviet Hind helicopters with engines roaring and massive dust clouds billowing under them wove slowly over the village. From time to time the sharp cracks of automatic weapons fire could be heard. Akil fainted.

The scant few survivors gathered in the cratered remains of the village, near the communal well. The Soviets had been thorough. Scarcely a wall over two meters stood standing. They shot up anything that could hold water, leaving only a few dozen pots, pans, and a handful of plastic water bottles. They gathered these at the well and began lowering a weighted plastic oil jug down into the dark hole.

The water they brought up was pink in color. The Soviets had thrown the bodies of children down the well to pollute it. It was all they had to drink. After that Akil only drank water at room temperature, or strong sometimes sweetened tea that he made himself, or watched others make. The imagined taste of blood lingered on his tongue for over two decades.

One of the survivors knew Akil and his family. There was really no other choice: Akil followed along until they walked out of the valley and over two towering ridges to enter the next village. There lived the aunt and uncle of

Akil's father. Several of the injured did not survive the trek. Their lives were marked by a pile of stones under which they were laid.

Life was always harsh; extreme heat, extreme cold, extreme terror as the mujahedeen fought with the Soviets.

There was never a good day.

## 31

Neah Bey studied the reports and made dozens of notes, mostly mental.

The agency or arm of the government that Neah worked for simply did not exist in any way, public or private. No budgets were voted on, no hearings administered over by temperamental will-o'-the-wisp politicians. It was the under-government that people suspected existed. It was the consortium of the business world and the world of the bureaucrat. It was the world that did not have many, if any, elected officials.

## 32

Indeed, it was the world of career bureaucrats and the members of the boards of directors of about 15 companies that ran the world. They dismissed presidential elections as scantly more than window dressing to appease the masses. It was a world measured in euros, dollars, yen, rubles, and little more. They held the view that what was good for business was good for everyone.

What had been rumored coming from Antarctica was

not going to be good for business. Whispers in shadowed corners sent micro spikes and dips on the world's stock exchanges. Tantalizing bits of data appeared and disappeared just as quickly.

The Committee of Business, also known internally as the Trade Group, or TG, became concerned when they finally amassed enough data to realize that something truly dangerous existed. Rumors were run down, people questioned, but there was only so much Business was able to do. They called the Smiths.

The Trade Group liaison had been to the Smiths before. A few years had gone by; she still traded brief emails with her old mentor. She typed out a simple "MSY" email and sent it along. It was scarcely a secret code for "Must See You." It worked; the return email identified a time when she should show up at the Smiths' near the White House.

Her limo arrived within the very narrow time frame identified in the email. The doorman, which he wasn't, did not help open the door or help her get out of the car. His attention was fixed on the open gate leading to the street. He held his hand up indicating that she should remain in the car until the heavy gate slid closed. When it slid into the deep recess of the bricked column he waved her on.

There was the usual ear piece with coiled wire running down under the heavy coat he wore, made even a little bulkier because of the protective vest. He stepped aside, allowing her to access the palm print and retinal scan devices. In all the years she had been around him, they never spoke; she thought she heard him being addressed as "Tex" on one occasion, but was never really sure.

Upon entry to the foyer she was met by more of the Smith receptionists. This time there was a pair of them viewing her from opposing sides of the room. It was always a little unnerving being under such close scrutiny. A door lock clicked, and one of the doors nudged open a little. One of the receptionists, a man who looked like he had been breaking rocks with his face, nodded toward it. She walked stiffly toward the door, entered, and closed it behind her. A loud sigh of relief came from her. The rigid wood chair looked inviting.

## 33

Budd Todd stared at the data again and again. It just did not make any sense at all. Using a variety of means, he layered the data, sifted through it, scanned for heat, some minor chemical traces, and sat back in the chair. "What am I seeing?" He went from narrow view to wider view and ran the data again and again.

The colonel wheeled over, having lost both his legs to an IED. "Well, Meat Head, and WHYFUN?" WHYFUN was an acronym for "What have you fucked up now?"

Budd Todd stared at the colonel, "Don't know, Wheeler, just got this data in and can't make shit out of it."

The colonel pushed forward and scanned the data, "Hmm, I see, very interesting, remarkable in a way."

Todd looked sideways at the colonel, "Err, you see something here I don't? Sir?"

The colonel smiled broadly, "Oh, hell no. But I got two tickets to the indoor rodeo tonight! Let's get shit-faced!"

Budd Todd laughed, "Let me just screw my legs on and let's go!"

The colonel and Todd had both been injured in the

same attack; they lay side by side for weeks healing from their injuries. The colonel called for his special van to be brought over to the funny door off the baggage handling facility, and they were off.

## 34

Ruby La Push began detailed note-taking on Dr. Dayton Astoria. She collected bits of his life on video and sent that along with her commentary to Mrs. T. Ruby discovered DA, as she referred to her subject, liked Rice Krispies for breakfast, two pieces of fruit and a lump of cheese for lunch, and pizza by the slice for dinner.

Dayton Astoria's small apartment was somewhat Spartan; everything was tied to utility over appearance. Possibly ten seasons in Antarctica had jaded him on certain refinements. On the ice, it all had to be packed in, and it all had to be packed out. Ruby drew a sketch of the apartment and developed a tracking program to trace DA's foot- prints through the unit. This she kept to herself and had not informed Mrs. T about it.

She would, in the dark hours, play the little program over and over, retracing DA's steps. After several weeks it became apparent that DA rarely if ever went to his small bookshelf. Indeed, the footfalls indicated that at times he actually sidestepped to be just a little further away from it.

Ruby used the camera system to zoom in on all the large text titles and noted each one. Mundane copies of academia, a cook book that appeared to have never been opened, some students' doctorial treaties custom-bound, and a rather shabby copy of *Journey to the Center of the*

*Earth*, rather fitting she thought, considering his career was spent drilling holes into the planet. The resolution of the cameras was not sufficient to capture all the detail Ruby would have liked.

Ruby's view into Dr. Dayton Astoria's office and lab at Central Washington was as modest as his living accommodations. Everything had a useful purpose. There were some high-powered microscopes and the usual Bunsen burners and the like here and there. Nothing extravagant, nothing out of place.

Oddly, the only thing that was out of place at Dayton's home or office was a very out-of-date periodic table, which hung from the wall in the office. According to Ruby's research, the chart should have contained at least another twenty elements. It wasn't until a few weeks had passed that the purpose of the chart was clear. A student brushed up against the chart causing the thumb tack which held a lower corner down to fall. Apparently to save money or time the area under the chart was not painted. Ruby has been hoping for something more unique than the State of Washington scrimping a few pennies.

## 35

They sucked down a few beers on the way to the arena. Talk was small and infrequent, and rarely about their injuries. The colonel had been and still was single, Todd had a fiancée, but that ended shortly after his return. He did not blame Traci; it was just going to be too much for her to cope with, half a man, shortened life expectancy, the constant adjustments to his *artificials*. It was not going to be zip lines, kayaking, and parasailing in Cabo, but an endless routine of therapy, pills, depression, and possibly more surgeries.

He was sad, but he understood when he read the note on the kitchen counter top.

Well, here they were front-row seats for the indoor rodeo! The indoor arena floor had just been tilled to a smooth texture when the gaudy rodeo clowns threw open a gate and a dozen bucking broncos frantically dashed out in all directions. They kicked, snorted, and flailed about, exciting the crowd to their feet. The gate opened again, and the horses dashed pell-mell for it. The clowns slammed the gate closed, and the announcer began introducing the current rodeo royalty. A fine collection of pretty women stood and waved at the crowd.

The colonel and Budd Todd stared at the tracks in the dirt. Their eyes never left it. It was an eerie replication of the satellite images they had seen an hour ago. Wild dispersion from a central point, then an orderly return to the same point. They sipped their beers slowly, tearing apart in their minds step by step, image by image, footprint by footprint. It all made sense, except for the heat tracings two hundred yards distant from the central point. That was solved when they had their van brought to the handicapped entrance of the arena at the end of the rodeo.

Budd went around making sure the colonel could access the wheelchair lift. In the cold Rocky Mountain air, the stall sweepings were very pungent, and steam rose from the pile indicating the warmth within. Budd turned the colonel around so he could face the pile and said, "Bingo, Colonel, Bingo." The colonel nodded.

## 36

Akil sat in the cave staring at the laptop monitor; he was being directed to lead one of his cave-dwelling associates to a meeting of Taliban and ISIS leadership. He resented the notion that he should have to lead someone as unimportant as Rahman to the meeting. That work should have been that of a child, or a woman.

Akil told Rahman to be ready in the half hour, and they would sneak away at dusk, even if the damned American's satellites were overhead. Two people would not be seen as a threat or even noteworthy.

## 37

Half a world away, a team of amputees had been working furiously for three weeks on what had become known as the Shit Pile.

Budd Todd walked somewhat timorously into the conference room. He was wearing his dress uniform with the medals and ribbons splashed colorfully across his left breast. The artificials clicked a little as the mechanical joints tried to replicate human anatomy.

Around the table were three generals, an admiral, and a half a dozen men in dark suits. One woman. A few heavy-hitters circled in the darkness, a security umbrella for the suits, Todd imagined. The colonel was seated at the head of the table in his custom wheelchair. "Ladies, Gentlemen, with great pride I introduce you to Captain Budd Todd, United States Marine Corps."

Budd was taken aback. One of the suits stood and said, "Captain, we acknowledge your service, your heroism, and your sacrifice made on behalf of this country. Please proceed." The suit's face leaned forward into the light; it was the Secretary of Defense. "From this moment forward, we are on a first name basis in this room, no titles, no ranks, no bullshit."

The Secretary motioned toward a podium, "Budd, time is critical, so throw your punches fast and hard."

Todd stammered, "Yes, yes, Sir."

The colonel winked at him and curled his index finger quickly: a signal from the other side of the world, remembered still, "Shoot to kill." Todd began.

"Taking advantage of the new satellite launch, I played a hunch based on previous data and altered the orbit of Condor." One of the generals tipped his head slightly. "I mean, I call it Condor, it's one of my space birds, sorry."

The general smiled and said, "Continue."

Todd stared at his papers for a moment and then realized he had yet to turn on the displays around the room. Views of the world flashed across the screens, some Mercator projections, some infrared, and some real time lookdowns of topography.

"I had some readings that I could not understand, some heat tracings that were unusual, some evidence that a cave system existed." He flicked through some images showing the mysterious heat image in the gully, then the image of the rodeo arena floor.

"I found one of our tech guys; he took these pictures for me showing how prisoners leave a single door in the exercise yard at the start of the outdoor period. You will note that everyone heads in a different direction immediately." He overlaid the footage of the exercise yard at Folsom Prison, and then overlaid the horses leaving the gate. "When the exercise period ends, you will note that there is a singular column formed nearly every time. I called my former case worker and asked her about it, she referred to it as 'first out-last in'; sort of getting the last gasp of freedom, or the last gasp of fresh air."

More slides slid across the screen. "Here you will see the faint heat tracings taken on a very cold morning at two different time intervals, one is the rapid dispersion effect of wanting to get away from everyone else, and the next is the singular column to delay going back in." More images appeared and disappeared. "Here I used this picture to track individual heat traces that might represent individual's footprints. You can see that there are approximately 75 to 85 individual tracks. Some are much separated; some are nearly on top of each other. It would imply that the individuals are single males and possibly leaders; the other closer traces are mothers with children or someone aiding an elderly person, or couples, possibly married."

Heads nodded around the table.

"Well done, Budd, what else do you have?" the Secretary of Defense asked.

Todd looked down at his notes, "I, hmm, have the feces calculation as supporting evidence?" The men at the table could hardly suppress their mirth.

The single woman cast disapproving glances to her left and right, and then said, "You mean the Shit Pile, as this place is known?" More giggles followed. The woman's immobile face finally gave way to a smirk.

"Well, yes, ma'am, the Shit Pile. I took these images of the, the, err, pile of shit, and referenced them to an older

66

view of the area. Using NumWon, I got the cubic volume of the area."

The lady leaned into the light and asked, "NumWon?"

Todd blushed again, "It's what we call Captain Lorraine, "Number Wonder," because of her math skills. I took the cubic feet of the feces and went over to the Denver Zoo and chatted with the Primate Director. It was fairly simple to assume that since chimps are pretty much digestively akin to humans, the cubic footage would support the 75 to 85-person population over three years."

"You said three years? How close to three years can you get?" It was one of the generals.

Todd scribbled some numbers on the back of one of his papers and quickly tabulated them, "I'm guessing six months, if there was no use of the cave prior to that."

"Two and a half to three and a half years? I think that's in the ball park." The general looked around the table.

The lady at the table smiled, seemingly like a shark smelling blood in the water. "I agree. Let's hammer this place."

The Secretary of Defense came over to Budd Todd and extended his hand.

"Major Todd, job well done."

Todd's eyes widened at the misstatement by the Secretary, he stammered, "But, I'm, I'm really only a Captain, sir."

The Secretary of Defense looked back at Todd and said, "Not any more, *Major.*" He turned his back and walked away. The colonel motioned that he and Todd should leave the room. A vee of sweat outlined Todd's shoulders. One of the heavies opened the door for the two men and stood stiffly at attention until they had passed through. Under his breath he whispered, "*Semper Fi*, brothers."

One of the generals leaned forward and said, "You

know the story about that kid? Lost both legs below the knees, used his belt and that of a dead Marine, put on his own tourniquets, and proceeded to shoot the shit out of everything in sight until he passed out from blood loss. The Medics had to pry his fingers off his gun to get him in the chopper." He took a breath and continued, "The colonel, that mean son of a bitch, although you would not think that to look at him, passed Todd ammo and used a sidearm to protect their six. High body count. Very high body count. Not that we do that sort of thing in these civilized times."

There was a brief silence, then the lady spoke, "The colonel doesn't use artificials to walk around?"

There were some smiles and smirks. "Well? What does that mean?" she asked.

The Secretary of Defense spoke, "Begging the Chairwomen of the NSA's pardon, he said the artificials chaffed his nuts." Even in the dim light her face could be seen to redden.

38

---

Rahman carried the paperwork that was less than useless to all but a few people. He had one small fragment that could be a tipping point, if it made it into the right hands. Between the papers and the fragment existed a possibility, a likelihood that for the most part an extinction-level event could be crafted, could be exploited. But just for those parts of the world he hated most, from those that he could profit most. He basked in an imaginary glow of adoration from the masses.

## 39

Akil was at the portal waiting. He did not like Rahman in the least. He got the best sleeping alcove, the one furthest from the buckets of urine and feces. Rahman was always deferred to with reverence and veneration that Akil felt he did not deserve. Akil suspected that Rahman had linkage to higher ups in Al-Qaida, the Taliban, and most recently, ISIS; however, Rahman was never seen to use a computer, a cell phone, or any communication devices at all.

Still, there was a constant stream of visitors that came and went. These all seemed to speak privately with Rahman and no one else. Many rumors were heard in the cave that Rahman was more than just a minor player on the world stage. By mere happenstance, Rahman and Akil could have been brothers. Several times Akil was addressed with salutations from visitors that meant high rank, but these were withdrawn when Akil corrected them.

Finally, Rahman appeared with a small woven bag that contained something hidden by the simple string closure. The cave opening was uncovered and both men exited into the dusk. About ten meters away Rahman stopped.

"Here." He handed Akil his bag and stepped back toward the cave entrance. Akil became angry that he was being treated as a servant holding the master's baggage. He turned toward the rising moon. With the sun fading over the mountains to the west. Rahman entered the cave.

Something caught Akil's eye. A sparkle of light in the early evening. He thought their journey was being blessed by the sight of a falling star. Such was not the case.

## 40

A modified Popeye Cruise Missile had been launched from a United States submarine that had entered undetected into the Gulf of Oman. It lay on the sandy bottom for three months at a time, awaiting orders. It rose like a leviathan from the cold depths until it lay in the warm surface waters. It got to a satisfactory posture and listened for the launch order.

Radars across the region did not detect the missile's launch. The Popeye was an Israeli cruise missile that had been significantly modified at sea by the crew of the unnamed submarine. The crew wore no uniforms, carried no Navy ranks, and if asked, simply said they were underwater technicians serving oil and gas platforms offshore.

Longtime members of the United States Navy talked secretly about the mysterious "other Navy," but not enough information had come to light. One sub captain said "They may have told you that they retired the *Grayback*, or the *Florida*, or they were using them for oceanographic research, but I don't believe them at all."

Private conversations amongst captains recounted short message bursts that told them to abruptly change depth and direction or forbade them from certain areas of the ocean. They speculated but did not know.

## 41

The Popeye raced low across the Gulf of Oman and then started the jinx-dance across the plains and then into the mountains of Afghanistan's Hindu Kush. It stayed low in the valleys, finally rising up over a mountain, and then began diving toward the cave entrance to the west.

With its part of the mission completed, the sub sank back down to within a few yards of the bottom. Enveloped in the darkness of the deep ocean, the sub drifted along with the sea currents. When it had drifted a few miles, it settled into the muck of the sea floor and began waiting for the next call to action. Hours later, an ELF signal was received, taking an hour to transmit and be received, it utilized the still operational system employed by the Indian Navy: JWD, SD. *Job well done, Secretary of Defense.*

## 42

Akil saw the falling star come closer and closer, and a moment of awe was replaced by fear. He dove to his left as the heat blast from the engine washed over him. Horror-struck he watched as the missile entered the cave. The echo roar of the engine in the confined space funneled outwards toward Akil. There was a moment of silence, and then a rumble, as a concussive wave knocked Akil down the hillside, which was what saved his life.

A column of fire, molten metal, vaporized rock, and human remains bolted from the cave. Small rock slides cascaded down the mountain. Akil rose to his feet and saw that tons of rock had collapsed down the front of the mountain, closing the main entrance to what had been his home for the last two years.

He scrambled around the back side of the ridge and knew that there would not have been any survivors.

Portions of the rear entrance had been melted by the explosions, which had been collapsed in a manner similar to the main entrance. Faint rumblings and small quakes assailed his ears and his feet as fuel stores erupted beneath him and corridor after corridor collapsed in the cave network.

## 43

Rahman downloaded the last of the data and shoved it off to his thumb drives. It was a very small netbook computer that he kept hidden from everyone. He then withdrew the hard drive from his netbook and pitched it into a small cooking fire. The protests of the women fell upon deaf ears; he simply could not be troubled by a little bit more or less smoke in the stinking cave.

He had read the entire message and understood, here was the dagger to stab into the heart of the Western world. For Rahman it was not about faith, beliefs, higher powers, or any of those notions. It was always about power, and money. He placed his passports, tickets, a little money, and credit cards into his bag. Seated on a small stool, he ran his fingers over the bit of metal that was so important. Using a small magnifying lens, he could just make out the remaining symbols. At some point this sample had been broken from a larger piece.

It was all he needed, this small fragment of metal and the data that was in his bag. In thinking about the probabilities for success and failure, he stopped placing the metal bit into his bag. Having all his treasures in one spot was alien to his thinking, it made for a single point failure.

Rahman fully understood single point failures and how one smart bomb or cruise missile could take out the entire leadership in one area. *And that is why I work alone,* he smiled, *and that is why I don't let more than two people meet me at one time. After all, being under the radar as they say, you live longer.* He tucked the metal part into a small pocket sewn into his clothing.

Rahman and Akil left the cave together. A few yards away, Rahman remembered that he had not said good bye to the elder that had arranged his hiding so completely. He handed his bag to that useless clod Akil a few meters from the cave. He felt at least a minor obligation to be polite, which was not his nature.

He told Akil to wait, which gave him a moment's pleasure at the obvious hatred Akil had for him. Smiling at his traveling companion's discomfort he walked slowly toward the cave entrance just to make Akil's impatience simmer even more. It was a trifling indulgence to torment another human being; Rahman savored every slow, methodical step into the cave. He turned to see if Akil was any redder with anger. He did not see Akil at all; he saw the ugly snout of the Popeye barreling into the cave. He was the first to die.

## 44

"God damn! Right on!" The general leapt to his feet. Real-time, look-down images rolled across the huge screen. They had tracked the mission from the small spark in the Gulf of Oman to the video image taken by the Popeye as it entered the cave. It was so mesmerizing in detail that several of the audience leaned left and right as the missile flew through the canyons of the Hindu Kush.

"Can you imagine what that one towel head at the entrance thought? There won't be enough left of him to fill a berry basket at Safeway!" The group exchanged handshakes and pats on the back.

"Well, Mrs. NSA, what do you think?" one asked.

The Chairwoman of the National Security Agency stared at the screen and said, "Sad that we had to exterminate women and children to get that prick, but in the end, it was the right thing to do." She forced a smile onto her face.

## 45

Akil had been burned, either by the exhaust wash of the missile or the fiery burst from the cave. It did not matter. He was at least a two-day hike to the nearest village; he had no first aid supplies and no water.

Taking Rahman's cloth bag, Akil was ready to throw it over the first cliff he came to. He sat down and stared at the thick tendrils of black smoke coming up from cracks between the rocks. He knew that the smoke was coming from burning human beings, he had seen and smelled it before. Akil looked at the bag and prepared to toss it over the edge. Thinking it might have some dried fruit or bread in it, he stopped and untied the string holding it together. For Akil, the universe changed.

## 46

Neah Bey began formulating a plan. Dr. Dayton Astoria would have to be dealt with sooner than later. While Astoria was not a direct physical threat to the United States, he was a threat to the status quo. The Smiths and others speculated on his findings. Sir Ernest Shackleton's secret diaries that resided in the basement of the Smithsonian alluded to strange findings on his failed expedition.

Roald Amundsen made quixotic references to things in the rocks privately, but never mentioned any of it to anyone other than close, trusted confidants.

In 1947, approximately two years after the close of the Second World War, the expedition led by Gerald Ketchum, United States Navy, had far more than just exploration on their mission profile. The diaries of the failed Robert Falcon Scott expedition were discovered adjacent to their bodies and returned. There were similar odd comments about mysterious things in the rocks. The Ketchum Expedition, called Task Force 39, consisted of 500 men assigned to Operation Windmill. Not all of them were studying the ice.

## 47

Captain Malaga stared at this watch; the second hand seemed to move slowly in the bitter cold. He shivered and nudged his second in command. Lieutenant Bucoda groaned. "So soon?

"Fraid so, Bucky, we gotta roll. The United States needs unsung heroes, and today, that's us," Malaga quipped.

Bucoda grinned, "You think there'll be dancing girls and a ticker tape parade for us when we get home?" Malaga laughed, although at this temperature, breathing in large amounts of frigid air could actually be painful. The select group struck out on their own. Racing by dog sled across the ice, they found the Scott expedition's final resting place. Here they meticulously sketched and photographed every aspect of the site. When that was accomplished, they dismantled it all, searching every pocket, every fold of skin, every container, and every square inch of the surrounding area. After careful examination, they restored the site.

From there they headed toward the interior. If something went wrong, as it often did in Antarctica, they would be on their own. They had no flares, no radio, nothing to call for help. They would just simply be lost, and that would be that. The dogs pulling the sleds appeared to pick their path very carefully, seeming to sense the half ton of high explosives they hauled.

Malaga rode, and one leg kicked from the back of his sled. Bucoda alternated jogging and riding. What had been brought back in 1948 was carried directly to the President, Harry S. Truman. After several days of contemplation, Truman ordered the material to be preserved and then conveniently "lost" in the bowels of the Smithsonian.

The only things shared between Malaga and Bucoda were Ph.D.s earned at Cornell and the University of Illinois when they were 16 years old and had a penchant for staying in excellent physical condition.

## 48

Kadar had been following the communications all along. He disliked the trashy Eastern European witch, Mrs. T. Still, means to an end sometimes had to be endured. His concern became great when Rahman fell off the radar. He had to use a circuitous route to get boots on the ground in the Hindu Kush. What he had feared had come to pass. The Americans had, what was the expression? Yes, the patience of a saint when it came to tracking people down.

After three weeks he finally got eyes on the collapsed tunnel. They carried a few tons of rocks away from the front and back entrances. After about a week it was obvious that those who were inside the cave had not survived.

Kadar began to attempt to bring in the second team. It was too great of an opportunity to miss. What fate had taken away, he hoped it would return in some other manner. He had heard of other samples being held in the United States.

Kadar and others hoped this issue, coupled with the reality of the artifacts, would crush the faith of the West, damage all their governmental power, defeat the religious block that supported those governments, and shatter the image of anything more than the here and now in terms of the business world. Rahman had the data, almost all of it, but that did not matter much.

The spin-doctors of Wall Street and Hollywood would breed instant counter messages, would hire stooges to wear sandwich boards, and create sit-coms to diffuse the evidence. They had done it before; he had studied the famous McNamara Gulf of Tonkin newscast. With practiced sleight of hand and carefully crafted words the Secretary of Defense purposefully built a message that inflamed the war machine of the United States.

The movie *Wag the Dog* was his constant reference to others who were skeptical. The power of American media could not be underestimated at its ability to dodge, deflect, and counter. He pointed out that in a poll conducted during a recent election year, a vast majority of Americans would bomb the Arab country of Agrabah. His Arab friends would stare at him in bewilderment and ask, "Where and what is Agrabah?" Kadar responded, "Only in the Walt Disney cartoon called *Aladdin*."

Kadar watched the newsreel footage of the Chicago Democratic Convention of 1968. He watched the kids riot and shout, "The Whole World's Watching!" Of particular interest to him was the supposed ensuing "police riot" and the entrenched powerfuls' reaction to a cohesive youth. The shootings that followed in 1970 at Kent State of unarmed students were almost preordained.

Then something changed; Viet Nam ended. The world calmed down. Yes, there were Panama, Grenada, the Falklands, but until Saddam Hussein began his genocidal march to a hanging and Osama bin Laden's flawed attack, the world was fairly calm. Kadar dug into the foundations of these issues.

A common thread emerged. At every turn there were the same corporate names, the same powerful individuals' names, the same powerful friends. These were not of the government. These were of business. While individual fortunes waxed and waned, a cabal of business remained strong. Boards of Directors were voted in and voted out, CEOs' heads were taken, and new heads grown to replace them. Still, this thread remained. It was the General Electrics, United Technologies, Boeings, DuPonts, and more.

These were the companies that ran the world. And the singular point that kept them in the running was simple: there was always going to be a tomorrow. Kadar controlled Rahman, and Rahman had everything in place to end that belief that "tomorrow is another day."

Kadar had and then had lost the paper trail evidence as well as one trifling sample to bring the world to a new starting point. Some of his Arabic brothers suggested that he should kill himself for this failure. Kadar had countered, the evidence existed; it just had to be found again to make the plan complete. He pointed out that bin Laden had done more to make the entire world hate those of Arab descent simply because he misplayed the power. Privately Kadar referred to bin Laden as "Johnny One-Note" or the "'One-Hit Wonder."

Kadar, ever the student of history, made the point of bin Laden being the equivalent of the attack on Pearl Harbor. Without the continuity of effort, without the game plan for the second half, both were failed at the start.

Kadar politely mentioned at several secretive meetings the thought-provoking quote of Isoroku Yamamoto, *"I fear all we have done is to awaken a sleeping giant and fill him with a terrible resolve."*

Kadar preached that no single strike would crush the entire Western World, but a single strike of such a significant magnitude would create ripples that could be exploited at every level. This is what the plan was all about.

Each of the thousands of homes would stockpile food, water, medicine for multitudes of people. As the governments failed, the voice of the Arab community would speak, calling the frightened to hear the voice of comfort and security. As the other major religions fell back upon mystery and thin remarks about "having faith," they would have medicines for the here and now. As the delivery systems for food and water collapsed as infrastructure was shaken, the followers would have cool cloths for fevered brows and a bit of soup for empty bellies.

Islam would appear to be the answer, but that was just a cover story. Kadar wanted the power and nothing more for himself.

## 49

Neah Bey sighed and turned the computer monitor off. "Well, now what?"

Ione had quietly walked up behind him in the office above the woodshed. She did not want to bother Neah, but they had a social gathering to go to that evening. She startled Neah by asking "Now what, what?"

Neah turned and looked at his wife. "What would you think if you found out that humans had gotten to the brink of the industrial revolution tens of millions of years ago, maybe billions of years ago, and then failed so completely as to have virtually ended?"

Ione thought for a minute and said, "I suppose if that were the case, I'd stock up on food, water, guns, ammunition, medicines, and wait until the rest of the world fell upon itself." She looked out the window across the pasture and saw a doe and fawn nibbling at the willow branches. "I can't imagine how people would see this as a good thing. It would rather fly in the face of most religions, most governments, most of everything we believe."

Neah smiled and said, "I take it if I don't hurry and shower and shave, we will be late?"

Ione smiled, "Yes, I know you don't like visiting the neighbors, but they have been polite and not too nosey."

## 50

Akil used the fading sunlight to study the contents of the bag. It contained three passports, credit cards, some cash, and a handful of thumb drives. He knew by looking at the passport photos that he could pass for Rahman, or Abd-Al-Aziz, or Fahd, such were the names in which the passports had been issued. In a smudged envelope were airline tickets from Kabul to Riyadh to Amsterdam to Montreal. A piece of paper stuck between the tickets displayed what Akil thought were phone numbers. If any of this was going to be of any use at all, he would have to survive a walk across rough terrain with little access to food and water.

He rather liked the name Fahd; it meant "panther," a predator worthy of respect.

## 51

Ruby La Push tried to focus the cameras onto the bookcase in Dayton Astoria's apartment. The lens or camera setup was just not good enough to read all the titles or examine all the bits of this and that. She mentioned this to Mrs. T one afternoon when she brought Ruby some of her favorite things in the world, real Canadian maple syrup and blueberry jam, the very best grades of each.

Mrs. T suggested that she and Ruby leave the world of surveillance behind for an afternoon and enjoy a nice ride over to Lower Hadlock across Puget Sound; There they would eat at the renowned Ajax Café. It seemed entirely out of place for this to happen, and Ruby was intrigued. Still, Mrs. T had been very generous, so she accepted the invitation.

Mrs. T picked her up in a modest limo; heavy glass separated the two women from the driver. They chatted about everything and anything except Ruby's work. It was a nice drive, the scenery spectacular, a ferry ride, and a tasty meal at the Ajax Café. She dozed on their way back, Mrs. T pecking at a tablet computer.

When she let herself into her townhouse, Ruby went right to her computers. Call it a sixth sense, but she felt very strongly that someone had been in her home. Somehow the images in the apartment of Dayton Astoria were infinitely superior. She could zoom in on all the materials on each table, each window sill, and could capture incredible detail of everything on the tantalizing bookshelf that Astoria avoided.

Astoria had a mirror installed in the foyer of the apartment. When her new camera system was installed, Ruby found the mirror. Next to it was a small handwritten note that caused her to laugh until tears came from her eyes. The Post-it note was in Astoria's handwriting and had several numbered lines: 1. Shoes match? 2. Socks match? 3. Belt on? 4. Pants zipped? The list detailed everything that Astoria might be wearing and served as a checklist for his apparent lack of attention to his dressing skills.

She zoomed in using her newly acquired capabilities, and even though it was a reverse image, she could read over Astoria's shoulder as he worked at his computer.

## 52

Malaga and Bucoda studied the maps and took bearings of the prominent features. Navigation was difficult, maps were rudimentary, and wind-borne snow made staying on any course difficult.

In spite of the barriers to success, they came upon the outcropping. The summer sun, sporadic at best, along with the wind, had eroded the snow and ice, exposing the vein of material that was the concern. Bucoda snapped some pictures and began sketching the area while Malaga laid out the charges. Roping up, they climbed to the top of the rocky outcropping. Here they laboriously pounded holes into the rock. Two days of effort yielded a series of ten holes four feet deep. Into these they packed the explosives.

Fearing that the dogs might bolt if they were too near the explosion, Bucoda took both teams about a mile away and stood by in a gully of ice and snow. Malaga stood at the base of the outcropping and stared at the ribbon of material that traced across its face. Bits of metal protruded here and there. Some were slightly rusted; other pieces were shiny and clean. He reached out with a bare hand to grab a souvenir and then thought better of it. Captain Malaga was not in the Navy, Army, Air Force, Marines, or Coast Guard. Then again, like Bucoda, he wasn't really anybody.

He twisted the igniter and began shuffling down the sled track to put distance between him and the rock face. Bucoda was staring at his watch when Malaga appeared from around the pile of shattered ice and snow. "'Bout God damn time, jackass! You purposely are late! You must like it when I freeze my gonads off!"

Malaga smiled, "Yeah, but think, we are off to some sunny climate, and there had better be palm trees, sand, rum, and big-hootered women in abundance." The dogs fussed in their traces, the first to detect the sound of the far-off rumbling.

Malaga looked at his watch and shook his head. "They were off by 57 seconds on the igniter. Make a note."

Bucoda rolled his sled to the upright position and looked at the sky. "Think we will ever know what this is all about?" Malaga walked down his dog team, rewarding each malamute with a bit of biscuit, some pats, and some rubs.

"I'm thinking that the sooner we forget this, the longer we live." He whistled to his dogs, "Let's run for home, puppies!" The two men slalomed through the up-tilted ice pinnacles of a pressure ridge, eager to get back to the relative warmth of the main camp. Their departure was unremarkable, and they were hoping their return would be met with less fanfare than that. Bucoda felt the heavy bits of metal in his pocket, but his orders were slightly different from Malaga's. While Malaga was attending to the final details of running the fuse lines, Bucoda fulfilled his mission profile by gathering a minimum of seven metallic bits.

53

---

Akil's first test was passing through the first of many checkpoints set up to protect the airport in Kabul. He had hidden the other passports in his baggage, which at best one would describe as modest. If he had arrived looking like a scruffy country bumpkin, he would have been rebuffed at the first checkpoint. He used some of his money to get a shave, haircut, and some nice, but not too nice, clothing and accessories. Akil splurged on some black market Old Spice aftershave.

While he fit the image of a respectable businessman, he thought *No, no that would be a trigger.* He hit upon the idea he had flown in from Canada to attend to some family matters up north, the death of a loved one. The ticket stubs and return airfare clearly identified this as a possibility. He thought some good might come from the demise of his "family" he had come to know in the cave. While he did not grieve for Rahman in the least, he did enjoy a fine restaurant meal with Rahman's money in an atmosphere that did not stink of too closely packed humans.

The next day he bought a small inexpensive computer that at least had ports for the thumb drives. In a coffee shop near the airport he turned his back against a wall and plugged in the first thumb drive. In order to access the data, he had to come up with a password. He thought for several moments, contemplating what an arrogant ass like Rahman might use for a password. The files opened when Akil typed in *Rahman!* There were several files that used abbreviations for their names.

Four files were not abbreviated: Scott, Shackleton, Amundsen, and Ketchum. He read them in order. In the end, he ordered a gin and tonic, a double. Akil's head swam a little from the unfamiliar effects of the alcohol and the burden of what he had just read. With his new wardrobe and assumed identity, having a drink would make him appear "Western."

He possessed information that could rock the world of those he felt had plundered and subjugated the people of the Middle East. While everyone would be traumatized over the release of the data, those in the decadent West would have the furthest to fall. Outside an old man tugged softly on the halter of a worn out and equally old-looking donkey carrying a small load of firewood. "We don't have very far to fall at all," he said to no one in particular. Using Rahman's credit card, he paid for the meal and gave a small but fair tip.

## 54

There was brief euphoria when the Hindu Kush cave was destroyed, and then it was back to work.

The phone rang and vibrated on the nightstand of the Chairwoman of the National Security Agency. She answered, "Yes? It had better be important." Her eyebrows furrowed deeply, "Are you sure? No mistake? He lives?" She hung up and punched the intercom button, "Coffee, toast, and the car in that order." Within two hours she was in her war room with her top advisors, fuming over the data.

## 55

Budd Todd saw the colonel waving at him through the glass partitions. He walked over, leaning slightly on his cane. Some days the imbalance caused by the artificials tired his back out more than others, and in those times he used a cane.

"Back bothering you again?" asked the colonel.

"Yeah, some days yes, some days no. What's up, Wheeler?" Todd did not have to wait for permission to sit down, not in the way the colonel ran this part of the Tube.

"Hey, remember when we Popeyed the Shit Pile? Intelligence says we missed the target. I find that doubtful. But, here it is." The colonel handed over a sheaf of papers.

Todd leafed through them briefly. "Nope, can't be. It was a righteous kill. Solid."

The colonel nodded in agreement. "I concur. However, greater minds operating at less than peak efficiency have become distraught. When that happens, it all lands here for clarification. Take a look at it again with a fresh pair of baby blues and get back to me."

Todd smiled and gave the colonel the thumbs up sign. As he walked from the office, one of his artificials began to squeak a bit.

"How the hell am I supposed to think with that racket going on? Get some God damn WD-40 on those sticks before you rust up like the Tin Man! Sheesh, the audacity to mistreat valuable assets of the United States government is just the--" His voice trailed off.

Todd turned to the colonel with a raised eyebrow.

The colonel smiled and pulled an expertly rolled joint from his pocket. "You wanna get high?"

56

---

The priest walked out of the sanctuary and headed toward his modest living quarters at the rear of the property. There was a bite to the air, made even a little more miserable with the fog and light rain. A few more degrees, he thought, and there could be snow. Boston could be lovely at most times of the year, but not today.

A hand fell on his shoulder, "Please do not turn around, Father." To make the point something poked him in the back right over his kidney.

The priest nodded slowly. "I have no money." Whatever was in his back ground in a little more deeply.

"I know and don't care." was the response from the person behind him.

The priest spun first, hitting the arm that was holding a gun against his back. His right elbow caught his assailant on his left ear driving the figure backwards. In the darkness he could see the automatic pistol lying on the ground. "You picked the wrong priest to pick on."

The man leapt from the shade of the landscaping and open-palm slapped the priest, causing him to now fall back from the attack.

The priest leaned forward, faking a left hand jab and connecting with an uppercut. The man stumbled to one knee and grabbed a handful of dirt, which he flung into the priest's face.

Temporarily blinded, the priest cursed, "Why, you cheating cocksucker!" He dove forward and tackled the larger man. He brought a knee into the exposed groin.

Tex gasped in pain. "Such language for a priest!" He head-butted the priest in return. "And a cheap-shot artist of the worst kind!"

They lay side by side gasping for air.

Tex's groin hurt badly; a trickle of blood came from each of the priest's nostrils.

"So what brings you here? We try to keep the riffraff

out, you know." The priest used the sleeve of his vestments to daub the blood from his face.

"Work." Tex sat up, "Work that is very important, Wallace, very important."

The priest shook his head trying to clear his vision, "And the thought of just sending me an email did not cross that small brain of yours?"

"Seemed to be impersonal to do that." He stood and helped the priest to his feet. "Do you still keep a bottle of snake bite in your desk for medicinal purposes?"

The priest dusted his robe and straightened up, "It's been a rough month, so there is only a half a bottle left." Satisfied that he got most of the dirt off, he extended his hand toward Tex. "How have you been? Are you doing okay since Nemah passed away?"

Tex ignored the extended hand and gave the priest a hug. "Yes and no. Some days are okay; some days it's all I can do to keep it together. Can we go inside and chat for a bit?"

"That important? So important that you will cross the threshold of a house of religion?" The priest held open the door.

"Yes, it's that important." Tex stopped at the doorway as if held in check by an invisible force. He then slowly and with great deliberation stepped into the apartment.

"There? See? You made it and did not froth at the mouth or get covered with boils." He smiled at Tex. "I do believe I have two clean glasses and a bottle of some sort of brownish liquid that aids in conversation." He slapped Tex on the shoulder, "At least that's my story."

Tex nodded and cracked half a smile, "Nemah always enjoyed coming here. She talked about the services and the youth activities. She liked working with the kids mostly." He sat down at the table and watched as the priest poured multiple fingers of whiskey into two glasses.

The priest turned his back to set the bottle on the counter. When he turned back Tex held out his glass for a refill. "My, are we thirsty?"

Tex set the glass down and watched it fill. "You know, I wonder if I had been more active here that God would have spared Nemah. Maybe that's why she died."

The priest lunged forward across the table, anger causing his neck muscles to bulge out. "Put that notion out of your head right now! That is not how it works! Never has! Never will!" He set the bottle on the table rather than the counter. He looked at Tex, anger fading into sorrow; he sat heavily on the chair. "You guys had something special, something no one ever sees anymore."

Both men sat and studied the glasses and the bottle before them. Softly, the priest continued, "You of all people should know that." He took his collar off before taking a drink. "We both know; we both were there." Another sip, "Every time we watched guys that did it by the book, made all the right moves, wore all the gear, followed all the orders." He twisted the glass a little and watched the liquid roll around. "And still, and still they died. A lucky bullet, and they were gone."

Tex nodded his head, "I know. Anyway, Wallace, I have a question. It is not an easy question." He took the bottle and filled the priest's glass. "You'll need this, trust me." He took a coin from his pocket and held it in his fingers. "Let's presume, let's say, that this is an artifact, complete, precise, irrefutable, and verifiable."

Wallace looked at the coin and back at Tex. "Got it, where did it come from?"

Tex flicked the edge of the coin allowing it to spin across the table. It gave up its speed and finally fell over and stopped.

"Where isn't as important as when," Tex looked at Wallace. "And when is a big problem."

## 57

Neah Bey drove in the spring rain through Snoqualmie Pass over the Cascade Mountain Range and into Eastern Washington. The weather cleared as he started down the east slope toward Indian John Hill and Ellensburg. He was on a scouting mission to Central Washington State University, the employer of Dr. Dayton Astoria. His iPad with cellular internet connection gave him Google Maps with satellite imagery of the campus and residential areas. Ione and Neah both liked Ellensburg and generally made a stop at one of the fruit and vegetable stands along Interstate 90.

Bey pulled into a public parking area and adjusted the zoom lens of the camera built into the Thule rooftop cargo container on the SUV. The camera display was on his iPad that he left resting on his lap. From this particular vantage point he could look into Dr. Astoria's office in the Sciences Building. Bey worked the camera back and forth, smiling at passersby while recording the video to the SUV's built-in computer. On a whim he left the camera running and strolled around the campus.

Spring flowers were blooming, and the grass was already nicely greened up. He wandered off campus and got himself a latte at the Utopia Coffee House, a shop filled with students.

To his surprise, Dr. Astoria was sitting at a table with some students and a stack of maps of Mongolia or Northern Tibet. Bey nonchalantly wove through the students and stared at a picture on the wall. He was close enough to hear Astoria conducting a class for some grad students in the coffee shop.

Taking his drink, he wandered out and back toward the campus. Bey dumped the half-consumed drink in the trash and walked up the short flight of steps into the Science Building. Smiling to those he met, he stopped outside a doorway and knocked softly. The door was unlocked, and Bey entered.

## 58

Across the state in Ruby La Push's townhouse, a computer monitor beeped and came to life. Ruby heard the beep and looked at her wall clock. Astoria was not due back in his office for another 45 minutes at the very minimum. She toggled the monitor to life and brought up the images of the office that should have been vacant. Here was a man she had never seen before standing with his back to the closed hallway door. He was looking down at a pad in his hand. In a fluid motion that belied his grey and thinning hair, the man keeping his face down opened the door and was gone from view.

Ruby played and re-played the video many times over. At no time could she directly see the man's face, much less make note of any distinguishing features.

## 59

The sophisticated detector began vibrating the instant he crossed the threshold. He pulled it from his coat pocket. It flashed in his palm warning him that he had just stepped into room that was being surveilled. Bey left. He checked the detector when he was in the hallway and adjacent to the building outside.

It was only a few blocks to Astoria's apartment house, so he walked. When he got to the top of the stairs that led to Astoria's unit the detector started vibrating and flashing again. Bey kept his face earthward and backed away. Astoria was being blanketed with eavesdropping, installed by people that were very good at their job. Only his highly sophisticated detector picked up the electronic signatures of the equally high-end cameras.

Bey called the Smiths from his vehicle. "Our target is bugged at work and at home. By whom?"

One of the Smiths, this time a man with a gravelly voice answered, "Good question, we are unaware of parallel interests." This meant that the Smiths, who were aware of everything as they were on everyone's payroll, did not know of any other governmental agency having an interest in Dr. Dayton Astoria. Bey frowned as he began driving westward over the Pass. Such interferences with operations conducted by the Smiths usually ended in bloodshed.

## 60

Ruby studied the video tape of the grey-haired man standing in Dr. Astoria's lab space. She played the tape at various speeds, including the equivalent of one frame every five seconds. Nothing seemed to pop up as being helpful. With her eyes fatigued from about three hours of studying the snippet of tape, she leaned back in her custom chair.

"There has to be something there!" she said to the monitors and walls. For the last time she ran the tape. As her hand moved toward the off switch, she saw it. By increasing the magnification on the stranger's hand, it became clearer. It was nothing more than a lucky break. By increasing the magnification to the maximum on the device in the stranger's hand, it provided a fair mirror reflection of the mystery man's face. It was just a partial view of the face, but it was more than enough to copy and run through some software she had.

Ruby edited the image into a series of still shots and cleaned up the image as best she could. If someone knew this person, there was a good chance the man could be identified to her. Ruby made an email with a few of the better slices of video tape and sent that off to Mrs. T.

## 61

Mrs. T sat with her tablet in her hand scrolling through the data Ruby had just sent her. *Rahman lives?* To top that off, Ruby La Push sent her a snippet of video tape. *Rahman lives and Neah Bey is now involved?* She smiled. She was positive she was better than Bey.

Mrs. T stared at the picture so intently that she jumped when her phone rang. It was Ruby.

"Yes, Ruby, how are you?" Mrs. T stared at Bey's picture.

"I am just fine, Mrs. T! I was wondering though." Ruby waited.

"Wondering about what, Ruby? Is there something wrong?" Mrs. T was fairly confident that everything was okay with Ruby, considering the expense that Mrs. T had gone to.

"Well, the picture of the mystery man that I sent. As you know, I like to file things appropriately for future ease of access." Ruby waited again.

"Yes, Ruby, you are a dear person for keeping track of things. What is your question?" Mrs. T made a gun shape with her hand and pointed it at Neah Bey in the picture. Under her breath she whispered, "I will get you."

Ruby spoke in her ear, "I'm sorry, I didn't get that."

Mrs. T said, "Oh, Ruby, it's nothing."

"Well, I am calling to know how to file this for you on the drive for future easy retrieval. What would you like the file to be called?" Ruby used the hands-free device, and placed her hands over the keyboard, ready to copy Mrs. T's response.

"Yes, Ruby, we should continue to file things appropriately at all times. You may call this file 'Neah Bey.'" Mrs. T wanted to add "soon to be dead," but that seemed to be a little overdramatic.

"I got it, Mrs. T, this will be the Neah Bey file from now until the end of time!" Ruby laughed. "And thank you for helping."

"Not to worry, Ruby, you are very professional, and I am grateful! And again, thank you so much for your diligence and professionalism. Good bye." She set her phone down and stared at the image of Neah Bey, with her finger still in the gun shape. "Bang, bang, you're dead."

## 62

Neah Bey it is! Ruby made the file folder on her desk top and slid the images into it. Then she went out to the web and began a very, very detailed search for the man behind the image, this mysterious Neah Bey.

## 63

Budd Todd started from the beginning and ended with the video tape taken by the nose camera of the Popeye as it honed in on the cave entrance. The image was quite clear; someone had been standing outside the cave when the Popeye ran home. Todd played and replayed the videos, all that he had taken and all that had been provided from others.

He stared at the colonel, who handed him the disks. "Buddy Boy, ask not from whence these came, just be grateful that we got them. Do your magic." When now Major Budd Todd sifted through the files, it became very apparent that someone had wanted this Rahman dead for a very long time.

The name did not appear to be connected to anything he had been working on until he read the alias list for Rahman. Fahd meant "panther." Panther was the code name for the person identified as responsible for the attack on the Benghazi Consulate compound most recently. Later he was identified as the broker for the sarin gas sale to Assad, who used it on his own people. He was a high-ranking money man for terrorism, as well as a global planner and schemer. Todd entered the names into his computer and pulled up the bio on Fahd, Rahman, and Abd-Al-Aziz, who were all the same, but different. It was not uncommon to have covert operatives carry the same code name and to even be similar in appearance.

Saddam Hussein used body doubles to his advantage. Having this built-in distraction could allow for confusion in the counter-terrorism efforts. It was a deadly game of not only "Where is Waldo?" but "Which Waldo?" Todd pushed back from the console. "God damn it." He sighed.

"God damn what, peg legs?" The colonel had rolled in silently.

"Ah, this chase. Rahman, Fahd, et cetera, all looking the same but not the same. I have a hunch that this is not Rahman; it is a photocopy person; it is a different person. Close but not the same. Having difficulty proving it." Todd stared at the monitors as images processed through a slide show.

The colonel tapped Budd on the arm. "Hey, how about we take a break at the titty bar?" Todd nodded. He was pretty sure it wasn't going to help, but then again, he was also sure that it wouldn't hurt.

## 64

Ruby set the computer to record everything. Her life became a mirror image of Astoria's. From time to time she sliced a section of video out and reviewed it over and over again.

One afternoon Astoria entered his campus office and uncharacteristically closed and locked the door. He then closed the blinds on the large windows. Ruby triggered the special recording program. Astoria tried the lock on the door and then went to his small collection of books. Behind one he extracted a key, the key unlocked the desk drawer, inside the desk drawer was a safe.

Astoria opened the safe by using a key that hung around his neck under his clothes. He pulled out a small metallic object. Ruby La Push zoomed in on the object and recorded the images. Astoria sketched the figures that were on the object again on a tablet, then placed the artifact in his pocket, opened the blinds, stuffed the tablet inside his coat, unlocked the door, and left.

Ruby La Push began studying the image; this became an obsession for her that she was not wont to share with Mrs. T for the moment, or if ever.

## 65

The Trade Group had many questions, so she as the liaison made the call. She sat in the straight-backed chair; the lock clicked, and in walked her old mentor and one-time one-night fling. It was the right thing to do at the time, but the wrong thing to do again. She had no regrets. Neither did he.

He remained single, and single of purpose, as she was also. He tapped the desk top. "I fear that you are correct. Our research conforms to your postulations."

She did not smile, "My, such eloquence from you."

He sat back, "Yeah, no matter how we slice it, we're just plain screwed." An awkward silence surrounded them. Finally, he spoke up. "So far no one mercifully has access to anything that at the present time cannot be written off as conspiracy-theory ramblings. If the artifacts show up in the hands of any astute scientists, then no bets. Our predictions suggest a cataclysmic degradation in government and business, the essential roles of most religions become obsolete, and society itself fails." He paused. "I wonder if this conversation was not already held sometime in the past." His fingers traced over the desktop images.

It was her turn to speak, "Do you really think that people will be that damaged? Do you really think society is that fragile?"

He glanced about the rather sterile room, possibly looking for some sort of stimulus which he could build an answer around. "I fear that rational thought would not be the strong suit for most of the world. To simply say 'oh, what the hell, so what?' I think is a bit of a stretch. At the very least there could be years of tumult. Years in which our enemies could play upon fear and uncertainty until humanity decides that it either will rise above this or fail again."

She waited respectfully, not having heard him utter so many words at one time before. "I, for one, think in a more forward-looking manner. Okay we failed, we tanked, we lost, but I look out the window and do not see failure. I see success from a failure."

He tilted his head to one side. "We are assuming that humans failed because of themselves, yet what if it was something else? Plague, meteor, war, aliens, and that list is endless."

She knew he had been an avid reader of science fiction. "Crazy Eddy?" It was a reference to an interesting story about a far-off alien civilization that endured, in fact counted on rising from its own ashes time and time again. "You think we can't do that again?"

He frowned. "Not with nukes in every corner of the globe. When everyone goes home to protect their loved ones, only those without love will be in charge."

Again a contemplative pause. "That bad? You think it will be that bad?" A note of incredulity seeped into the corners of her voice.

"Well," he brightened, "We can stall and hedge and corral as best we can. If we can do those things, then maybe by the time this gets out humanity will be better able to process the facts."

She glanced toward the desk top, trying to see what he was reading upside down. "Am I to guess that you have, what's his name? Bey? Working on this?"

He nodded. "Wouldn't be the first time that the future of the world rode on his shoulders."

Smiling, she asked. "Isn't he like, you know, old?"

It was his turn to smile, "Old? I'll take a guy with a humanity switch any day."

She rose to leave. *Yes*, she thought, she had heard that Neah Bey could murder men, women, and children in the morning and yet remembered to bring home flowers for his wife in the evening. Some day she would like to meet the infamous Mr. Bey. She also wanted to meet his wife; she must be something else as well.

As she waited for Tex to let the limo into the courtyard, she reflected that her mentor had related that he feared two things: drowning and having Ione Bey be mad at him. Something about shooting a priest to death after he blew up her house. She was going to press the issue, but declined as the frown lines appeared around his eyes.

## 66

Now Mr. Fahd, as he preferred, lived alone in a hotel unit just outside the city center in Montreal. He jangled the flash drives in his pocket. They had revealed much information. The late Rahman was more than what he appeared to be. As a senior advisor to ISIS, Taliban, Al-Qaida, and organizations he had never heard of, Rahman had connections everywhere. And enemies as well. It was a bit of a shock to see that most of his enemies were the true believers of Islam that wanted to rid the world of pretenders like Rahman. Those that twisted the faith and the minds of far too many.

Revealed in the flash drives were bits and pieces of a mystery. It seemed to indicate that humanity had started over. He felt his soul seemed to understand that getting proof of this theory would be a greater blow to the West than any series of 9-11 attacks could bring about. His personal mission was to acquire the artifacts at any cost and display them for the world to see.

It would be the strength of his people that would shrug this off and the weakness of his enemies that would push them over the edge. He smiled at a pretty young woman that was paying him some close attention. Such tawdry couplings served no purpose other than to mask his purpose, but he only partially believed that.

## 67

Neah Bey edged around the apartment complex in Ellensburg and acted like the meter reader he dressed as. In a few moments he had spliced in the tattletale and was gone. He had set the tattletale to send packets of information at odd times. They would appear to be scant more than bits of static to anyone else.

Three days later he began to go through the files that had arrived. Someone was watching Dr. Astoria with great interest.

## 68

Ruby La Push was too involved an observer to not notice the minor glitches in the system. She began to investigate the random little chirps of static. It became clear that someone was now watching her watch Astoria.

She became intrigued and started an operation of her own. She and Colton made a trip to Ellensburg. They placed one of Colton's readers adjacent to the tattletale installed by Bey. As they used canes and walkers to cross the frozen grass, Colton began laughing loudly. Ruby stopped, "Here we are committing a felony, and you start laughing. Are you nuts?"

Colton could hardly contain his mirth, "We look like an American Disabilities Act and an Equal Employment Opportunities ad for spies!"

Ruby raised a cane menacingly, "Don't forget a woman scorned!" She waved the cane at Colton.

When they got to Ruby's car, Colton rubbed the still visible bruise on the side of his head, and muttered under his breath, "Bitch."

"I heard that!" As the car doors closed they both began laughing, a nervous release of emotional energy at best.

It took time, but she managed to piggy back onto everything Astoria was doing. She copied all of his files onto her own machines and then slid those copies off to a special place within her private laptop. It took months of watching and waiting.

## 69

Dr. Dayton Astoria read and re-read the email several times. It had no address, no identification at all. What technology had produced it he could only guess. Yet, here it was. It said "You have something we want; you will give it to us, or suffer."

## 70

Ruby La Push watched and waited. She had been told to pay strict attention to the life of Dr. Astoria starting at 12:35 p.m. Saturday. Why the time frame was so specific was rather an interesting puzzle. However, for the moment she did as directed and watched. Using the upgraded software and cameras, she could look over Astoria's shoulder as he read the email. He, in turn, looked over his shoulders as if feeling that he was being watched all the time. She wondered if he sensed the cameras.

Astoria stood up and walked with great deliberation toward the bookcase. Ruby gasped. Astoria grabbed the bookcase and slid it to one side. Due to the weight of the materials on the shelves, two of them buckled. The well-organized and rather fastidious Astoria ignored the damage and scattered books. Behind the bookcase was a smooth-finished, sheet-rocked wall. Astoria kicked the wall with his foot, causing a hole to appear about three feet off the floor. He knelt and pulled some fractured sheetrock away, enlarging the hole. Reaching into the cavity, he pulled out an ore bag and dumped the contents onto the hardwood floor.

This was what Mrs. T had told Ruby to watch for, Astoria revealing the location of something very important. She was on the phone before Astoria grabbed a hat, coat, wallet, keys and placed the materials back into the bag and was gone. Mrs. T thanked Ruby for her efforts, and asked her to continue looking for Dr. Astoria at his home and office, knowing that the likelihood of his visiting either place was remote.

71

---

It was a gamble, but with Neah Bey assigned to this case, drastic action was warranted. Mrs. T had crafted the email herself, hoping to inspire a fight-or-flight reaction.

It worked. They had a tracker on Dr. Astoria's car and even his mountain bike. She typed in some commands, and Google Earth opened up, showing the location of the bike at the Science Building where it was chained and a moving dot heading south from the campus toward the freeway to Seattle.

She fired up her tablet computer and began tracking the vehicle from it. First she had to stop by Ruby La Push's townhouse. She had a few loose ends to tidy up; one was to send her counterpart in the Middle East a message. She attached every scrap of information that she could, along with several of her and her colleague's opinions as to the usefulness of the information and how it might be utilized.

## 72

Fahd, a name that he had indeed become more enamored with each day, stuck the last of the flash drives into his computer. He suspected it was more of the same, cryptic jargon about contacts, endless copies of emails that meant nothing to him. Sometimes there were files of music, and very surprisingly, more than one file of decadent pornography. These usually contained graphic nudity and marked hatred for women and children.

He did not understand why a person who appeared to be so focused would come under the influence of such debauchery. Fahd was not a fool; he saved what he did not understand for fear that it had some hidden content.

There was one massive file, about fifteen gigabytes that he opened last.

Fahd did not stop reading until he finished the entire

file. With stubble bristling on his face and the dry rime of sweat on his collar wearing into his neck, he looked at the clock. He had been reading for an entire day. Fahd sat back, stunned. Rahman was more than just an imperious oaf; he was a leader, a planner with such a view of the world that few could rival.

Fahd took it into his mind that he should follow through with Rahman's work, not for the memory of Rahman, but for the fame it would bring himself. He became smug and self-serving; after all, fate had selected him to carry the contents of the woven bag half way around the world and had de-selected Rahman with the missile. How could he refuse such a task that was handed to him by clearly a higher power?

## 73

Mrs. T knocked softly at the door, knowing that Ruby was already waiting there. It was a matter of courtesy that she always called when she was a few minutes away. This allowed Ruby to secure her machines and adjust her braces and canes and be in route to the door. "Well hello, Ruby! May I come in?" She smiled broadly.

Ruby shuffled aside and said "You bet, Mrs. T, you just come right in."

Mrs. T patted her on the arm holding the door, "You are such a dear to be here. Let's go to your office and chat."

Ruby closed the door and said, "Sure, you know the way, and would you like some coffee?"

Mrs. T shook her head, "No, no thank you. As they say, I have miles to go before I sleep. I can only be here for a few minutes, just thought I'd swing by and see how you were doing."

Mrs. T pulled over the second chair in the office, not the special one that Ruby used, and sat. "Well, wasn't that exciting when Astoria kicked open the wall? Who would have thought he would hide something so completely?" She smiled again.

Ruby saw that strange wrinkles were at the corners of her eyes and mouth. "Yes it was very much a surprise; however, I did mention that it was odd he never went to the bookcase, and seemed to be avoiding it. Very suspicious if you ask me." They both laughed.

Ruby turned to the computer, "Here, just a second, let me end this program." Ruby's fingers flashed across the keyboard. The computer screen went dark. The usual hum from the multitude of machines went silent one by one until just the faint murmur of the wind against the glass panes could be heard. Ruby's laptop on the shelf behind her did not shut down like the others.

"I was wondering what you thought that particular monitor over there was like, you know, if it was easy on the eyes or not?" Mrs. T nodded to one of the larger displays.

Ruby turned to look at the last electronic glow of the over-large monitor, "You mean that--" she was unable to finish the sentence, as Ruby La Push was unconscious. Mrs. T, using nothing more than a Burger King drinking straw as a blow gun, placed a dart in the back of Ruby's neck.

"Well, thank you, Ruby, you were a great help." Mrs. T pinched the dart making sure it had delivered all of its contents into the still form and placed it in her purse. She then punched a speed dial number and waited. The connection was made, but no one answered. "Clean up here, tear this place down immediately. Leave the girl as you find her, but gut the systems." She turned the thermostat on the wall up to 90 degrees.

Mrs. T knelt by the side of Ruby La Push and lifted her shirt up. Ruby had tried to keep it a secret, but she used an insulin pump to control her Type One diabetes. Mrs. T quickly detached, drained, and refilled the pump with an incorrect dosage. By the time the incapacitating narcotic wore off, Ruby would already be comatose and unable to self-rescue. With the heat in the room elevated, Ruby would burn off the narcotic long before any meaningful medical assistance would take notice. This would also further dehydrate and exhaust the young woman. Death could take a day or more, but it would still come.

With a final glance around the room for loose ends, Mrs. T left.

## 74

One of the numbers in the information Fahd received had a small star next to it and a date. Fahd called the number from a pay phone in Vancouver, Canada. The phone rang three times and then was answered.

"You are not Rahman." Kadar spoke.

"I have become Fahd, and I am better," replied Akil.

Kadar thought for a moment. "What makes you better?"

"Rahman only wanted to destroy; I want to do that and one better." Akil waited, a tactic he emulated from the late Rahman.

Kadar paused and then felt compelled to ask, "What is the one better thing?"

Fahd swelled with a bit of pride; Kadar had been forced to beg the answer. "I want to lead our people to where they should be, an Arab world, a unified world, and our world!" He hung up the phone, smiled, and retired to his favorite night club to see what came of the evening. His world view was very simple: it had him as the leader.

## 75

Ruby La Push was no fool. Her typing skills would give her a life after death. She had no delusions that what she was doing was highly illegal. She also surmised correctly that the people she was working for would do anything to keep it a secret. Ruby La Push exploited resources within the computer network she was attached to. She hoped she could play her poison pill to keep herself alive.

Even though she did not know him, she felt that Neah Bey might be her only friend in the world. She was clever enough to make a dead-man email, or in this case, she smiled inwardly, a dead-woman email.

## 76

Ravenna Lakota shifted through the files that Bey had sent her. She too had access to a highly sophisticated computer system like Ruby La Push.

The phone rang in the SUV. "Hello, Babe," Neah answered.

"Yeah, 'Babe.' I should tell Ione that you talk to strange women like that." Ravenna laughed. "You buy me lunch at Ephesus in West Seattle, and I'll keep a secret."

It was Neah's turn to laugh, "You are most certainly spot on with the 'strange woman' idea. They just don't get any stranger than you!"

"Oh, well, enough of the pleasantries. I'm sending you a map with the location marked for whoever is recording Dr. Astoria. If I am correct, and very much unlike you, I always am, you are about five minutes away."

"You are the best! Thanks." And with that the conversation ended. A map already locating him on a GPS screen flashed up on the SUV's rear view display.

77

---

Bey drove by, scanning the front, and then looped through the alleyway and back to a side street. Using the rear-view mirrors to check his six o'clock, he appeared to fumble with a map. It was a quiet suburban street. Nothing untoward seemed in play. He got out and walked down the passageway toward where the utility and services part of the townhouses were placed. There were some telling features on one unit. An overly large exhaust stack protruded from the garage area. Further investigation revealed a bundle of cabling coming out of the cable TV box, not consistent with a single-family dwelling.

Neah pulled out his lock-pick gun and within seconds was in the door. He drew the .45 from his waist band. He began to duck-walk down the hallway. There was a door that was open by only a scant half inch. The floor plan was mostly open, so he retreated and worked the perimeter back to the door.

There was a wave of heat coming from the room off

the entry. Using the tip of his shoe, he slowly pushed the door open. Ruby La Push lay face down on her keyboard, eyes partially opened and glazed. He stepped back and surveyed the scene before him. Young female, partially disabled from some accident or illness, complex computer system that appeared to be turned off. He spotted it on closer examination, a slight welt just above the hairline on the girl's neck. Neah checked for a carotid pulse, not really expecting one. To his surprise, he could feel the faint pulsations of a beating heart. He called Ravenna.

There was an internal stair Bey investigated that lead to the garage area. The generator and battery system was designed expertly, much like what he had at home.

He returned to the office area and sat in the chair he assumed the assailant sat in. Mentally he began a checklist of what he saw. Something did not add up. Why was the computer off? He pushed the chair closer peering over the young woman's shoulder. He touched Ruby's hand and moved it from the keyboard. A monitor flickered to life. Words, one character at a time began to appear on the screen. "Who are you?" Neah pulled the .45 from his waistband again. He listened intently to the sound in the room, in the townhouse, in the street. Nothing exciting or disturbing.

Neah pulled the keyboard from under Ruby's hands. He typed in "ME." The screen defaulted back to the question, "Who are you?" a number one appeared, followed by two blank spaces. He sat back, then found Ruby's purse. He typed in "Ruby" and again the screen defaulted back to "Who are you?" and a 1 and a 2 appeared with only one space left.

*"Well, what's the worst that could happen?"* Bey thought

for a moment. He typed in 'Neah' and the computer flashed, "Neah who?" He typed in "Neah Bey." All the monitors sprang to life.

The central one displayed an image of the young woman who lay face down on the desk. "Hello, Mr. Bey. I know all about you." The image paused.

Neah smiled, "Didn't know I had a fan."

As if responding to his statement, it continued, "And if I know all about you, so do they."

He called Ravenna again, wanting an update on her arrival.

Neah carefully cradled Ruby La Push in his arms and carried her to her bed. With the tips of his fingers her closed her eyes and gently covered her torso with the comforter. Then he waited in the darkened townhouse for someone to kill. He did not have to wait long.

## 78

Perry sat in his parents' front room and idly chatted with his mother and father about his work. He had to be rather cagy in talking about working for NEST. It could be very difficult for Perry and very dangerous for his parents if anyone knew exactly what he did.

Three weeks before they had intercepted a message that the parts of a dirty bomb were being assembled in Central Africa; it was in the possession of an African arm of ISIS. Perry had all the requisite skills to handle the mission. He was smart, young, and tough.

Randle was jealous at first. "Why would they send a stick-boy like you into the danger zone when they could

112

send me? I am clearly more handsome and would therefore make a much better poster-child than you."

They laughed. Randle shook Perry's hand and said, "KLAG, my friend, KLAG." It meant "Keep Low and Go." Perry promised to live up to the low standards set by Randle at the agency family picnic where Randle successfully struck out all three times at bat.

Randle rolled his eyes and said "And to think I paid you to shut up about that." The rest of the team at the coffee table tried not to grin or laugh too much.

Within thirty-six hours Perry stepped off the transport plane in Monrovia with his small team and disappeared into the jungle for three weeks. He came back on a special military transport with a lead-lined box in the cargo hold and with far fewer arrows than he left with.

79

Within the hour, Ravenna Lakota showed up with a group of the Smith, LLC, cleaning detail. Neah motioned with his head to where the computer was located. The cleaners were also paramedics, among a variety of other useful skills. They fairly pushed Bey out of the way as they ran to the aid of the stricken young woman.

Ravenna set up her Pelican cases and began scanning and downloading everything.

Eventually, the cleaners took care of the two dead men in the foyer. Neah stood by the bedroom door. The taller of the cleaners approached and spoke softly. "Don't worry, Neah." He peered at his fellow cleaner, "I, we, we will be respectful. I promise. I think," he paused, "we think we got here in time. When we figure out what the welt is from and the state of the insulin, we can start treatment." He patted Bey on the shoulder, "It just may take a very long time."

Neah looked into the room at the prone figure under the down comforter. "I'd appreciate it, really." He slid sideways to allow the man and woman cleaning team to enter. With a heavy heart he went to help Ravenna.

## 80

A file arrived on Neah's computer detailing the short but interesting life of Ruby La Push. Ravenna called in the afternoon to say that she had cracked the encryption of Ruby's files that were separate from the main files. The files were encrypted with a Latin phrase, *"Liberata mai."* "Save Me."

The brightness in Neah Bey's soul dimmed upon hearing that. He felt that he may have failed a remarkable young woman who had faced hard challenges. That part of him that was eroded away was replaced by something far more sinister: the need for revenge.

## 81

Budd Todd and the colonel worked many hours trying to refine the image from the Popeye. Who was the man that potentially survived the missile attack? They filtered, refined, changed algorithms, and edited existing software to help them. Nothing seemed to work. The colonel began flexing his muscles not only in the United States, but around the globe. He was provided access to terabytes of video footage from subways, shopping malls, airports, street corners, and more.

On these he and Budd utilized multiple facial recognition software suites until they had exhausted all the local resources and foreign outlets. The colonel then called up the Secretary of Defense; it was time to call in some major support. The Secretary's Admin was a bit put off that some heretofore unknown colonel was calling upon the Secretary of Defense of the most powerful nation on earth and began explaining that to him.

The colonel said into the receiver, "Hey, Dip Shit, do as you are told, or I will make public, and write this down, something to do with the Caribbean. Got it? Walk your butt into the Secretary's office and say, 'Call Wheeler, or the Caribbean issue is made public.' Got it, you ass-clown?" The colonel hung up.

Budd was leaning against the colonel's door. "Err, sounded more like blackmail than a request for assistance, begging the colonel's pardon for eavesdropping."

The colonel smiled, "Nope, screw that. That tit-less secretary is already in his Holiness's office trying to act important. He will be lucky if he is still employed tomorrow. We shall wait to see how long it takes for the phone." The colonel smiled, as the phone rang quietly, "Well, wasn't that awfully prompt?" He motioned that Budd should leave the room and close the door behind him on the way out. Budd lingered a little and heard the colonel shout, "Hey, just kidding, really! But while you are on the line." Budd decided that he should leave on that note and went back to his cubicle to sort through more data.

## 82

Fahd began attending prayer services at a nearby mosque, not to participate in the rituals he despised, but to aid in his cover story. If he was going to succeed, he was going to need some allies. One of the flash drives contained what appeared to him to be names with postal codes. He searched for and found a mosque that was almost dead center in one postal code near his hotel.

## 83

It took far longer than he anticipated to gather his artifacts, erase files from his computer at his office, and secure university equipment properly. At last Dr. Astoria drove slightly under the speed limit across the mountain pass. He felt rather alone and directionless. At this point he had no idea what he was going to do. The ore sample bag that contained the evidence of the end of the first human civilization kept catching his eye. Pulling over in the chain-up area on the east side of the pass, he stopped and placed the bag in the trunk, hoping it would be less invasive to him. Thus protected from distraction, he picked up the pace a little.

## 84

Mrs. T watched the blip on her smart phone draw ever nearer to her location. On a ridge outside Preston she nestled into a prone shooting position. Using her familiarity of the pass and the surrounding environment made this a good spot. When Astoria came around the corner, the setting sun behind her would be in Astoria's eyes. Most people would slow down when blinded by the brilliant light. It would be over before he knew what hit him. She began to pace her breathing.

## 85

Ravenna Lakota called Neah on his cell phone. "Whoever is watching over Astoria has a bug in his car. I predict much badness in this."

"Okay, not the best of news. Where is Astoria?" Bey stepped on the accelerator, and the heavy SUV bolted up to one hundred miles per hour. After the success and enjoyment of the pickup truck, he had his brother-in-law modify the government-issued SUV.

"I have him west of North Bend. I also have more bad news." She tapped on the keyboard in rapid strokes. Had he not been distracted by the call, he would have enjoyed the throaty rumble of the big V-8.

Bey frowned, "How bad?"

Ravenna pecked at the keyboard and sent a real-time satellite image to Bey's screen. "I think this is a shooter." The combination video and heat image showed a prone figure lying in the brush about a mile ahead. A parked car was still radiating engine heat about two hundred yards from the figure.

"Damn, how close is Astoria?" Bey did a quick check of his mirrors for police vehicles.

Ravenna had been doing the calculations in her head. "You have less than a minute to interrupt the shoot."

Bey pressed the pedal to the floor and fed a little nitrous oxide into the carburetor. The digital speedometer rolled off the numbers hitting one hundred and twenty-five in just a few seconds. Bey hit the sunroof switch. As the roof retracted he pulled out the heavy .45.

Ravenna placed a dot on Bey's vehicle to identify his location in respect to the shooter and Astoria. With horn blaring he slid sideways down the gravel shoulder of the Interstate. Traffic was mercifully light.

86

---

Astoria took his foot off the gas as the sunlight blinded him as he came around the corner. After all these years of traveling between Ellensburg and Seattle, he chided himself for once again forgetting about driving into the setting sun. The windshield fragmented into a thousand shards.

87

---

She had calmed her breathing and practiced holding a bead on the joint between the neck and shoulders of drivers coming toward her. It was going to be easy. She tried to ignore the random sounds of engines on semi-trucks pulling a little harder coming up the grade from her left. A horn was blowing, possibly someone venting a little road rage steam at another driver. Splinters of Douglas fir and bits of forest duff erupted around her. The shooter was close, as there was hardly any delay between the impacts and the sounds of the muzzle blasts. "Damn," she whispered to herself as Astoria came into view. She tried for a snap shot and watched the windshield disintegrate. The last shot from the freeway shooter nicked the top of the scope. She rolled to her right and was on her feet running toward the car. She did not look back. It wasn't until she got into her car that she realized she had been wounded.

### 88

Astoria slammed on the brakes and lost control. Acting like a bulldozer blade in the soft soil of the freeway medium, the front bumper buckled. He was knocked partially senseless when the airbag went off, which threw his forearm into his face. The car ground to a stop after blowing a tire when it hit part of the guard rail. Traffic noise assailed him, horns honked and tires shrieked. He fumbled with the door release.

### 89

Bey emptied the magazine from the .45 into the brush around where the shooter lay. He winced when the heavy rifle blast came from the brush.

Ravenna shouted in his ear piece, "They are running toward the car! Go get Astoria; I'll watch your six."

Bey cranked the wheel over and cut across the Interstate. A cloud of dirt and tire smoke obscured Astoria's car. He punched the automatic four-wheel drive button, and the SUV's tires bit into the soft median turf. In seconds he was at Astoria's car. He reloaded the .45 and walked toward the car where a dazed Astoria flailed about inside. The door was locked, so using the butt of the semi-automatic, Bey broke out the window and unlocked the door.

"Dr. Astoria?" Astoria nodded in a confused manner, still somewhat disconnected from having gotten punched in the face by the air bag. His nose and lip bled. Blood was welling through his shirt in a few spots. Bey's strong hand grabbed him under the shoulder and began pulling him from the car. "Doctor, we have got to go, now." Astoria tried to pull away from this stranger. Bey jammed the gun into Astoria's xiphoid and pulled his head down so he could see the gun clearly.

"I don't have time, people want you dead, and if you don't come with me right now, I will be forced to shoot you myself," Bey growled.

Astoria nodded in acceptance, still unclear as to what had happened. Bey pushed Astoria towards the SUV, "Where is the package, Dr. Astoria?"

Astoria tipped his head toward the car and mumbled, "Trunk, in the trunk."

Bey pushed the man towards the SUV. "Get in, now." At the back of the car Bey tried the trunk lid; a single shot from the .45 popped the lid open. Bey grabbed the ore bag and walked to the SUV. Astoria was in the passenger seat fumbling with his seat belt. A siren wailed in the distance. Bey jumped in and somewhat mindless of approaching traffic crushed the accelerator to the floor and hit the N02 button. Fire and black smoke erupted from the straight headers under the rear end.

The SUV leapt to over a hundred miles an hour in a handful of seconds.

"Ravenna?" Bey concentrated on his driving. Astoria was mumbling about not having his seat belt on and why they were driving away and something about his windshield breaking.

"State Patrol pulled over at Astoria's car, no pursuit at this time. The shooter has left the area." Astoria began fumbling with the door latch, thinking in his confused state that bouncing down the Interstate at one hundred miles an hour was better than being abducted.

Neah pushed the very warm barrel of the automatic against the doctor's temple. "If you want to die, that is a simple problem that I can fix. Keeping you alive is rather what we are all hoping for, Doctor Astoria."

Astoria froze in the seat, and stopped reaching for the door release. "How do you know my name?"

Bey had the SUV down to normal freeway speeds. He withdrew the gun. "Doctor, suffice it to say that you have a lot of enemies and damn few friends. I am one or the other, depending upon if you cooperate."

Astoria sank back into the seat. "Okay, I understand." He nodded to the ore bag between them. "It's about that stuff, isn't it?" Bey looked over at Astoria; he was rumpled, bleeding from several cuts on his face and neck. He looked every bit the absent-minded professor. In a way, Bey felt sorry for him, public life over, shot at, covertly surveilled, and the possessor of earth and society-shaking evidence that human life had come and gone before. He would have to restart his life in another field, in another name, and even possibly, in another face.

Bey turned his attention back to driving. "Ravenna? Anything on the shooter?"

Astoria turned to Bey, "Huh? Who are you talking to?"

Bey put his finger to the side of his head identifying the ear piece. "Ravenna?"

"Standby, Neah." Ravenna had hacked into the Washington State Patrol computer-aided dispatch system and began entering erroneous information on the suspect vehicles. "Okay, Neah." The earpiece chattered. "WSP is looking for people and vehicles other than you. I have tried to zoom in on the shooter. I have nothing to report. Is Astoria still alive?"

"So far." was all Neah said.

"Understood. Are you in possession of the artifacts?" Ravenna asked.

Neah asked, "Dr. Astoria, this is very important, and I need you to focus for the right here and the right now. Got it?" Astoria nodded his head. "Doctor, is this the complete collection of Antarctica material?"

Astoria glanced at the bag. "If I say yes, I die? If I say no, I still die?"

Bey nodded his head to the affirmative. "Your best bet is to tell the truth, give us something to work with. In this line of work, there is just the now, with no promises for tomorrow."

Astoria thought for a moment. "That is all I have with me." He sighed, to some degree at least for the moment his statement was true. "But I suspect there is more."

Neah spoke, "Yes, we suspect there is more as well."

Astoria's chest fell in a little, "You mean the Shackleton, Amundsen, Falcon, and Ketchum rumors?"

Neah nodded again. "So far they are just rumors. We

are running to ground those items. What do you know about the Truman Directive?"

Astoria grimaced. The Truman Directive was Astoria's Holy Grail. In his research he had tracked down all leads, all hints, and all the conjecture.

## 90

"Well, that is a heck of a statement." Wallace, the priest took the coin from the table and let it roll down the back side of his fingers. "Are you sure? Really sure?"

Tex nodded, "Yes, this appears to be legitimate, without equivocation."

Wallace took a sip and then drained the glass. "Okay, so you and I would simply carry on as if nothing had happened." He took the coin and put it in his pocket. "I think a rational person would say, 'Who cares exactly when humanity started?' Yes, it is important, but how does it impact me?" He looked at his empty glass and continued, "The fact that evidence exists that explains that we were off by a few million, or even a billion years in understanding when human beings started to act civilized, well, again, how does it change my daily routine?"

"Are you going to give my coin back?" Tex stared at the pocket where his coin now resided.

"Well, no." Wallace the priest smiled back, "It's mine now." Wallace listened to the rain lightly fall on the roof. "What are going to be the key issues here are easy to dismiss in the minds of those who are smarter than say, a cucumber." He took the coin out of his pocket and put it in another pocket, just to irritate Tex some more.

"I fear that there will be two issues in the minds of people. One, people will get really mad that governments have lied for more than a century." Wallace rose and picked up a tablet computer and quickly typed in a search request. "Well over fifty expeditions were launched to Antarctica prior to the mid-1950 era." His finger traced over the data, "Japan sent a team, Norway claimed part of it, as did Germany, Spain, and here's a good one, Belgium."

"Belgium? Why would Belgium go there?" Tex peered over Wallace's shoulder.

"Better yet, America sent two expeditions shortly after the Second World War. In order to pull off those two expeditions, planning would have had to occur while the war was still being fought. What could be so important to instigate that?" Wallace's fingers moved the data around some. "Operation Highjump was staffed by forty-seven-hundred men, and that took place starting in December of 1946. Clearly the Antarctic was high on everyone's list."

"Well, there were whaling and seal-hunting expeditions, but forty-seven hundred men taken out of the war effort is rather incredible." Tex peered at the data. "Fine, everyone wanted a piece of the action, but let's get back to the artifacts."

Wallace sat back, "You first said 'presumed artifacts' and now you're not saying 'presumed,' which would lead one to believe that such things exist."

Tex put his hand on Wallace's shoulder, "Tell me what you think would happen if they were?"

"I cannot for a second believe that everyone would shrug their shoulders and say 'oops.' As matter of fact, I am pretty sure the majority of the population would go bonkers. Their faith in the government," he swept his hand

124

across the page detailing all the countries that explored Antarctica, "heck, lots of governments, would be shaken." He sipped from his glass as Tex sat down.

"Let me paint a picture. We have preached that God created us in his image. He created the good and evil in the world. If that is the case, God has already let us, us as in the human race, die out, or so completely that the few remnants are meaningless at best. Why?" He turned the tablet off. "Most religions would have great difficulty in explaining why they should continue to believe, to have faith, in a God that decided to reset the game clock. And to be sure, reset the game clock completely. I, for one, do not think the story of Noah and the Ark is as far reaching as what you are proposing. And indeed that is a story that is not a universally held belief." He shook his head and took the coin out of his pocket again. "I am going to guess that the possibility exists that such artifacts are in fact real?"

Tex looked around the room, "You should keep that to yourself, Wallace."

"So, there we have it all." Wallace used his hands to take a wrinkle out of his collar piece. "Humans, according to our teachings, must have prayed to a God that forsook them. Completely, or nearly so."

The two men locked eyes for a moment. "This is not going to go over very well anywhere," the priest concluded.

Tex rose to leave. "I fear that is the case. At least until the human race can understand the distinction."

Wallace took the last sip from his glass. "Distinction? What are you referring to?"

"For the earth, for the soil and the sky and the water, for roughly four-and-a-half billion years, it has been here. Logic says that we should have a measure of *faith* that tomorrow will come again." He smiled, "I'll take a four and a half billion-year track record that there will be a tomorrow."

Wallace smiled back, "Yes, that would be a safe bet. However, there appears to be an argument that *we* might not be here to enjoy it." He slid his chair back and stood, "And evil would and will take advantage of the uncertainty."

They shook hands and walked to the door. Wallace put his arm around the large shoulders of Tex. "You know you are always welcome here, really you are."

"I know, and someday I might surprise you and show up. I'll bring the bottle." A limo was parked at curb. The driver saw Tex walking toward the road and started the engine. "Hopefully that will be under better circumstances than the last times I have been here."

Wallace stood nearly at attention and whispered, "*Fratres mei custodem.*"

Tex whispered back, "Always, My Brother's Keeper." It was the motto of a very special branch of the Department of Defense, which answered only to the President.

## 91

As he lay in the private room, plastic tubes running into his nose, the IV drip counted down by seconds the remainder of his life. He had much to be proud of. Fifty years of service to his country. He had lead black ops before they had the name in Viet Nam, Cambodia, Panama, and elsewhere. There were many places listed in a half a dozen passports that he could call home. In truth, it was always just another barracks, just another camp, and just another chunk of mean bush in some bug-infested war zone.

His honors were only sung in dark corners, he lacked a face, he lacked a background, and he had only a name spoken in great reverence in small meetings of a select few. Ghoster. A living legend. He smiled, and the nurse wiped a bit of phlegm from his lip. *Not so much living now*, he thought.

The nurse leaned forward and spoke into his ear, "Mr. Bucoda, you have a visitor. Would you like me to stay?" Bucoda rose slightly and squinted at the doorway. A youngish man stared back.

Bucoda lay back, "No, dear, it's all right. I know this man." He really didn't know who the man was, but he suspected that this was his time to die, taking with him secrets that could topple governments, crush businesses, end careers, and more. He was mistaken. The nurse left, pausing at the door to look over the young man, and then closed the door behind her.

"Thank you for seeing me, Mr. Bucoda," Dr. Astoria spoke softly. "I have something to show you." Astoria opened a portfolio and showed Bucoda the sketches that he and Malaga had made nearly sixty years previously. "Do these look familiar?"

Bucoda grimaced as a wave of nausea passed through him. All this time spent with chemicals dripping into him, and his stomach still revolted. He shuddered slightly. "Yes, Malaga and I." His voice trailed off.

"You and Malaga drew these in Antarctica in 1947?" Astoria pressed on.

Bucoda nodded slightly, "Yes." An arthritic finger pointed at the initials at the bottom of the page. Tiny meticulous letters "SB" and '47 were evident. He gasped and wheezed out, "I am Sloan Bucoda. Who are you?"

127

Astoria laid a hand on Bucoda's arm, "I am a man who knows what you found."

Bucoda closed his eyes, "And you have questions?" They chatted for many minutes.

## 92

A week later Sloan Bucoda slipped into unconsciousness with his favorite nurse by his side. He crossed over peacefully enough for a man with a past. Later, after the body had been removed by a detail from the government, she opened her purse and dialed a special number that had been memorized. When connected she tapped out a code of twos and sevens. The party at the other end disconnected the call.

## 93

A former President of the United States of America upon hearing of the passage of Ghoster sat heavily into the chair on the porch. The Secret Service agents stepped forward, unsure of what was happening. He waved them off. "Leave me. Leave me alone." He leaned forward resting his elbows on his knees. His fingers clasped together as in prayer. "You were the best of all of them."

The nearest agent whispered "Sir, sir?" The agent stepped forward a little, bowing down to listen to the former President. "Sir? Is there something…" His voice trailed off.

"I need to be alone for a bit. Back everyone off, now,

please." The agent stood and spoke briefly into his cuff mic. Quietly the agents took up different positions, taking care to not be seen.

The former President of the United States of America whispered, "*Fratres mei custodem*, my dear friend."

94

---

While researching the Ketchum Expedition, Astoria had found a cryptic remark about materials taken to the current President at the time, Harry S. Truman. He had nothing else to ponder at the moment, so he began tracking down the box that so interested the President. At first there were many dead ends, as boxes and files that old had a habit of slipping off the data base. Still, he liked ferreting out things; it was in his nature.

Over the course of many years he had run down dozens of empty boxes, file cabinets with no contents, dusty tomes of records that lacked relevance. All that he found was a hand-drawn sketch done in pencil by someone with the initials "SB." He slipped the sketch into a folder of papers and slipped from the room in the lowest level of the Smithsonian. Something about the sketch seemed unusual.

Time and many callous fingers touching the drawing had smudged it. He kept it and tried to figure out who SB might be. It was by no small coincidence that he chose the particular place to drill in the Antarctic. The Ketchum mission records were mostly complete, a little too complete in some areas, and considerably lacking in others.

## 95

Fahd strolled out into the park, the last of spring and the first of summer made it very pleasant in Montreal. He sat in the park and contemplated the clouds. An older man approached and sat next to him. They nodded a greeting to each other. In a few minutes the older man left, leaving a small paper sack between them. Nonchalantly Fahd picked it up and walked back to his hotel room.

## 96

It could only have been Bey. The man was either gifted or blessed with blind luck in abundance. She used a strip of nylon stocking and some fast food napkins to stop the blood flow from where a lucky ricochet sliced into her arm. In her Lake Union apartment, she numbed the area and put in five stitches herself. Not even a halfwit med school dropout would miss the fact that this was a bullet wound. And that meant the police, and questions, and more. That, she could not have. It hurt a great deal. With the setting sun glancing off the shimmering waters of the lake, she poured herself a large tumbler of her favorite wine and sat topless on the balcony. Her police scanner had informed her that there were no fatalities involved in the car wreck east of Seattle. Mrs. T began feeling the warmth of the wine seeping from her flat belly outwards. In the background her computer blinked.

## 97

The bag contained more flash drives, a few handwritten notes, and credit cards. Fahd tucked the credit cards away and then painstakingly etched to memory the email addresses on the paper. These he tore into small fragments and in a heavy shower flung them one by one from his balcony into the midnight sky of Montreal.

The flash drives contained everything he could have hoped for. It was the sum total of everything gleaned from decades of research. An end to usurious companies, an end to false gods, an end to the normalcy of the Western world and all its evil decadent behavior. All that it lacked to be the perfect destructive weapon was physical evidence.

How could you believe in a lesser god that had failed humanity before? Why take an interest in politics when proof existed that they had lied to the populace on countless instances? In some cases, for more than a century. Why abide by civility and law and order when the curtain could be drawn closed at any moment? Clearly being lawful and obedient did nothing to prolong the lives of the first human race. What would be the point of paying for anything when money itself was doomed? He laughed and shook his head from side to side. It was the greatest joke ever told, the doomsday preppers, the Y2Ks, the zombie apocalypse cadre, the followers of Heaven's Gate, well, they were right and wrong. They were right that the world was going to end; they were just wrong about the year and the manner.

Fahd smirked, *rather takes the utility of life and health insurance out of the market place.* And so would end the vilest corporations in the world. Chaos would reign, and he would be the answer. Fahd could take on the mantle of being an equivalent to an emperor himself. He would be revered throughout time, the Great Restorer of the Middle East. In his arrogance he thought he would fashion a new religion based on himself.

He hummed a little tune as he walked into the hotel lounge and ordered himself a drink. He would have preferred Bombay Revelation Gin; he thought that some measure of humility would be the better road, so he ordered a well drink instead. He sipped the drink and caught the eye of a red-haired beauty. He felt he was being rewarded for his good work.

On the flash drives were a biography and photos of Dr. Dayton Astoria and his approximate location. Also included was a file on some minion of the corrupt world, a Neah Bey. Fahd smiled not only at the redhead, but inwardly, pleased with the fact that his ascension to greatness was at hand.

## 98

Neah called Ione and informed her that they were going to have a house guest for a bit. Ione asked what she should prepare for dinner. Then she took her Sig Sauer .380 and tucked that into her waistband. The last time guests invited and uninvited came to call, most of her house was blown up, and she shot a priest to death in the front room.

Her cellphone rang again. It was her friend and associate of Neah Bey's, Ravenna Lakota. Ione was grateful to hear that she was headed to the house and would arrive about the same time as Neah and the mystery guest.

132

## 99

Mrs. T fumed; it was Rahman or it wasn't. Credit card usage was tracked from Afghanistan to Montreal. Her operatives had made contact, but their reports were questionable. The pictures they took when a package was passed on could be Rahman, or even more frustrating, someone that looked like Rahman.

And now, the team she had sent to gut the computers of Ruby La Push had not reported in.

## 100

The Chairwoman of the NSA sat back in her chair, fuming. The last half hour was spent getting browbeaten by the Vice President of the United States of America. In spite of his tenure as a Fire Department Chaplain for the City of Portland, Oregon, while serving in the state legislature, his comments to her about being "a stupid bitch" were stinging at the cellular level.

"Tell me again how this happened?" She could scarcely contain her anger.

The Secretary of Defense shrugged his shoulders, "Don't know, don't care, it's not the man, it's the mission. The Not-Rahman has the information. We have tracked him to Montreal. Here, watch the side by sides." He nodded to Budd Todd, "Roll it, please, Major." Todd entered the command. Side-by-side video footage began playing across the large monitor.

Todd spoke, "Rahman, Kabul 1999; Mystery Man, 2001.

Rahman, Amsterdam 2004; Mystery Man, police custody, Tora Bora 2005. Rahman, Kabul again, 2008; Mystery Man, Amsterdam 2013." Two still pictures froze side by side.

The Chairwoman of the NSA uttered a few unprofessional comments under her breath. "Okay, is Rahman dead or alive?"

Todd spoke up, "We believe he is dead. I present the following." A data flow showed information directed to and coming from Rahman. The flow ceased the day the Popeye entered the cave. Then a few weeks later, a few messages began again, limited in number. Todd offered, "At this point the assimilation of the Rahman persona by the surrogate began." Some heads nodded in affirmation.

"Here we find credit card purchases beginning. First in Kabul. Then on a layover at Schiphol. And in earnest in Montreal and the surrounding area." Credit card bills were highlighted and then expanded upon. "We have a personality change evidenced here. The Original, as we have labeled him, never purchased anything that did not support the overall beliefs of their cell. No alcohol, only modest hotels, and as near as we can tell he had one suit, and it was off the rack at best. Nothing was flashy, nothing out of the ordinary. BSC is not the same."

The room was silent. "Okay, I'm waiting, what does BSC mean?" Her gaze burned a hole through the center of Todd's forehead.

Todd's face reddened from neck to forehead, "Well, we call him the Bastard Step Child. BSC for short." This time no one smirked.

"Okay, continue, Budd." She spoke through a frown.

Budd highlighted some of the bills, a private tailor, a

134

high-end hotel, expensive drinks, room service, and night-clubs. "Either Rahman was struck by lightning and rein-vented himself, or this is an imposter. Someone has com-mitted identity theft on a high level player." Heads in the room sagged.

The Chairwoman of the NSA spoke up. "Well, we got Rahman, now we have his doppelganger, and we have to get him too. Does it appear that he has co-opted the mis-sion as well?"

The Secretary of Defense said, "It appears that this is the case." Heads sank a little lower.

The Chairwoman of the NSA asked, "Where is he now?"

Todd answered, "Vancouver, Canada." Video footage played out across the monitor; Fahd's face was circled as he walked down the concourse at Vancouver International Airport. The time stamp indicated the footage was taken less than ten hours ago.

## 101

Using the credit cards and newly received identifica-tion, Fahd purchased pre-paid phones at a Source Store in Surrey, British Columbia. Crossing the border at Blaine, Washington was uneventful. He called from a coffee shop near Green Lake, in Seattle.

## 102

Mrs. T did not recognize the number; usually she let it go to the messaging function. Since it had a Canadian area code, she picked up the phone and accepted the call without answering.

Fahd waited a moment and finally said "It is I, the Messenger."

Mrs. T thought and finally said, "You are not Rahman."

The answer came back quickly, "That is true, and the point would be?"

Mrs. T shot back, "Rahman is known, you are not. Why should we trust you?"

Fahd said simply, "Rahman is dead. And I am here with the data. I have everything that Rahman collected up until he died. Do you have all of that?"

Mrs. T sat back, "All right, you have the data. You are in. Let's meet."

103

Dr. Dayton Astoria was trying to reconcile his life. Ph.D. with Honors, University of Wisconsin School of Geology; single; ten seasons on the ice and in the mountains of Antarctica. His mission started while doing research on the early explorations of the icy realm. He was often called upon to supply appraisal work of bits of this and that which were thought to be memorabilia from the early days. The first days of investigating the Antarctic were often referred to as *the Heroic Age of Exploration.*

Leather gloves, boots, compass fragments, ships' equipment, and more, Astoria was something of an expert on the equipment hauled back and forth. Most of the time dating the artifacts ruled out their provenance. Still every now and then a musty relic was dragged out of a basement, an attic, or long-forgotten relatives' safe that was unique.

Dr. Astoria was sent pictures and samples of a variety of things over the years, and from these inquiries he developed an advanced knowledge of what it would take to survive on the ice. After he got his doctorate and was looking for a research position, an old friend from college called him up. It was an interesting assignment, only three months, but it would be going through some material from the Ketchum Expedition. He eagerly took the position.

He did not know it at the time, but his work was commendable enough that he was offered the same position on breaks from school and when his life on the ice did not interfere. For Astoria, digging through the relics in the Smithsonian was an excellent paid vacation he enjoyed for years.

Over the decades specimens got shuffled from here to there and back again. Uncaring or unwitting curators mislabeled boxes, forgot to catalogue the contents, or just simply wrote "MISC" on the box and found a conveniently empty shelf to place things.

Over time the call would go out to consolidate collections, send duplicates off to other museums, or hold fund-raising auctions of interesting but not germane antiquities. The task given to the young doctor was to sort through a vault in a sub-basement of the Smithsonian's remote warehousing facility and evaluate the material. Here lay an odd assortment of mixed materials, some from Shackleton, and some from the rest of the early explorations.

One befuddling condition existed that caused Astoria to waste valuable time; he called it "souveniring." An expedition from the late forties would gather materials from prior expeditions, and sometimes dozens of years would have passed from one expedition to the next. This created confusion in working with the relics that were at some point all thrown into the same box.

He was allowed to run his fingers through nearly a century of history on a place he hoped to visit. That was years ago; since then he had been to Antarctica ten times.

In a large chest with rusted hinges and no markings were some desiccated leather fittings used to shield the face and eyes from the intense sunlight reflected off the ice. In the chest lay a few hand tools such as a hammer with a rat-gnawed hickory handle, some chisels, a collection of rusty dinnerware, and a small box.

The box fairly disintegrated in his grasp. He used great care to transport it to the clean table. Under the multiple lights used to minutely examine objects, he carefully peeled back the layers of cardboard, leather, and concealing layers of heavily waxed paper. There were a few fossils, some small meteorites, and a few specimens wrapped in oily cotton or canvas. He picked at the fabric and extracted a nice set of fossils.

The next-to-last tightly wrapped bundle was different; it was heavier than stone by a substantial margin. It also had a small tag on it with the words "Site 2-4-47-SB" written in almost a calligraphy style. He carefully unwrapped the heavy object. A bit of shiny metal peeked out from the wrapper. The bright lights made it clear that the wrapper was at least sixty years old, but the metal fragment inside looked brand new.

Astoria used his trusty loupe to examine the artifact. Strange markings could be seen along one side. They were at once strange and at the same time familiar, not quite

English, not quite hieroglyphics, not quite Norse runes. Using white-gloved hands, he carefully turned it over and over in his hands. It did not fit in. He set it down, and his eyes glanced over the wrapping paper; it was a sketch of a rock outcropping.

A bit of paper was loose in the box. A label had over the years worked its way free of the specimen it was attached to. It had a date. It was a specimen from the failed Scott Expedition. A small journal, bound in leather, lay in the bottom of the box. He bundled up the more relevant items and slipped those into his pack sack. When he was finished reading the diary, Doctor Dayton Astoria went out and got uncharacteristically intoxicated.

When he returned the next day, five hours earlier than usual, he found the room had been completely cleaned out. He wasted no time in leaving with his prized possessions. Some of these he placed in a safety deposit box while on a layover to Seattle. The layover allowed him to rent a safety deposit box at a regional bank. The teller in Omaha was bored to death and far too busy playing with her smart phone to ask questions.

104

Kadar had used his position with the advertising firm to work his way across the Mid-west time and time again. He made many contacts, generally the owners of shoe stores, delicatessens, theaters, a cross-section of America in a cross-section of displaced Arabic people. From time to time he was invited to dinner at a client's home. He followed the traditional pattern of prayer and attended local mosques when he could. In some smaller communities they would meet in homes to discuss the Koran, politics, and more. In all cases, he and his followers used the faith of others for their own ends.

It was in Milwaukee that Kadar was introduced to Adiba, a pretty college student working to become a curator of antiquities back home, should there be any left after ISIS began destroying their common heritage. They exchanged pleasant emails from time to time.

He found the Somalis the most eager to talk to, and to plan with. Unlike most of the Iranians, Afghanis, Iraqis, and Saudis who had little use for the "African Arabs," whom they considered inferior and barely Arab, Kadar felt they were his best chance. Still they had a place and could be useful. He cultivated a few contacts within the group from Minneapolis.

There were three of them that had promise, no arrest records, and while affiliated with the Somali community, were more white than Arab in their features. Kadar had tracked other American citizens himself and relied heavily on information from back home.

The mujahedeen-wannabes were rarely useful. Most of the time they acted tough, promised the world, but right before boarding the plane to the Mid-East, their mothers would call and tell them to be home before midnight. Others were so deranged that they had to be sent on blind suicide missions. This was the least useful outcome. Basically these individuals were told they were carrying a suitcase of great importance to a high-level meeting. It would be remotely detonated by others. Problem solved.

Kadar had no interest in wasting his time with such low-level, halfwit enterprises. He wanted something more, something stronger, and something more decisive. Kadar sat back in the turboprop he was licensed to fly and adjusted his head phones.

He pondered how to take the Not-Rahman, this Fahd, his apprentices from Minneapolis, and the artifacts that Astoria held and craft his plan. He smiled inwardly. Fahd, Astoria, the witch T, and the apprentices; well, sacrifices sometimes had to be made.

## 105

The Smiths began to study the pertinent social and religious issues at hand. They had many people on the payroll; the first they talked to was the Rabbi.

## 106

Ione stood at the door when the remote driveway tattletale chirped. She watched the car come around the curve in the driveway. It was Ravenna Lakota; she always flashed her headlights three times when whatever she was driving passed between the two large cedar trees. Still cautious, Ione put her hand on the custom grip of the Sig. She relaxed when Ravenna stepped from the car and waved. At that point Ione began scanning the tree line until Ravenna stepped past her into the house. With the door closed they hugged and retired to the kitchen. Ione had the tea kettle on and laid a small platter of her honey-whole-wheat chocolate chip cookies on the kitchen island.

Socrates, the Rag Doll cat, felt obligated to jump on the countertop and bash skulls with Ravenna. He flopped down between the two women. They exchanged pleasantries.

Ravenna hedged around the issue of Neah. "So, how is Neah these days?"

Ione whisked some imaginary crumbs into her napkin. "I don't know what he is working on specifically, you know, security and all." She patted the 18-pound cat that stretched out begging for attention. "I was very worried about him and whatever he was working on."

Ravenna patted the big cat as well. "He seemed a little distracted for some time and then kind of gradually came out of it." Ravenna smiled, "You think he is okay now?"

Ione thought for a moment, "I hope so; he seemed to be his old self when you called him the other day."

Ravenna took a bite out of the cookie, "Oh, God, these are good, I'll have to hit the stair climber later." Another bite gone and then, "Neah will be fine. He got a little more wrapped up in things earlier today, but did fine. Do you know who he is bringing over?"

Ione said, "No, he seemed rather out of breath, a Doctor-somebody I have never heard of before." Ravenna maintained an emotionless face. If Neah wanted to tell his wife that he had been involved in a freeway shoot out three hours previously that was his affair. Their conversation would have to wait as the driveway tattletale chirped. Both women reached for their firearms and laughed at their shared reaction.

Ravenna gave hand signals that she would exit the rear of the house and take a position overlooking the driveway. Ione waited at the door, keeping an eye on the security monitor. It was Neah in the SUV, odd that the front end

142

seemed to be carrying long fronds of what appeared to be grass caught in the grill.

Neah stopped the vehicle and gave a quick scan to the tree line. Ione pressed a nail- head near the door, which caused a small green LED to illuminate on the ivy-covered stone wall. Neah looked toward the house and craned his neck around, trying to find Ravenna. He knew she was near, but just where was an issue. No matter. He walked around to the passenger's door and opened it for Dr. Astoria. A few wash wipes in the glove box had cleaned up some of the nicks on his face. Astoria stepped out and was motioned toward the heavy front door. Bey walked backwards, eyes looking, ears listening. The door creaked open. Ione stayed inside the entryway with one hand hidden behind the door.

She smiled toward Astoria and beckoned him in. "Hello, I'm Ione Bey. And who might you be?"

Astoria was taken aback by the smile and warmth of the greeting. "I'm, well, I'm Dayton Astoria." Ione extended her left hand to shake Astoria's.

Neah backed into the front door and hooked an arm around it and closed and then latched the door. Astoria stepped back; Ione Bey had a gun in one hand at her side. Neah Bey had a heavy semi-automatic at his. From out of nowhere an olive-skinned woman with jet black hair appeared, carrying a small machine gun.

Astoria flustered, "I, what, who, I'm . . . I'm not sure." His voice trailed off.

Ione broke the ice by sliding an arm through the doctor's arm and said "Tea and cookies?" She tugged his arm toward the kitchen.

Neah holstered his weapon and smiled at Ravenna, "Thanks, Babe, appreciate the overhead action."

Ravenna smiled, "No problem, any updates about the girl?"

Bey frowned, "She is in a coma and will be for some time. It is rather iffy at the moment, they tell me. Still don't get it, never will. Valuable asset wasted for what? Maybe I'm jaded or, or something."

Ravenna patted him on the shoulder, "Hardly, it's called having a conscience."

Bey cringed, "At my age? Rather unbecoming of a, of an, just what the heck are we anyway?"

She pushed him toward the kitchen, "Don't ask." Astoria sat on one of the high-backed kitchen stools with a cookie in one hand and Socrates' magnificent feather duster tail in the other. "So you guys are spies or something?"

Ione poured the tea into a clear glass cup. "Oh, my, no, just normal folks living in the country."

Astoria stared from Ravenna holding the machine gun to Neah holstering his automatic to Ione pouring tea. "Well, I might need convincing about that."

Ravenna stepped forward, "Dr. Astoria, I am Ravenna Lakota; this is Mr. and Mrs. Bey. Neah and Ione to be exact. Neah saved your life earlier."

Astoria nodded either in acceptance or disbelief. "I have many questions."

Neah said, "And so do we."

107

The Rabbi had been politely asked to the Smith, LLC, before. It was a little harrowing to be patted down, scanned, fingerprinted, and have a picture taken of his retinas.

144

He walked over from the synagogue. The tall man who stood guard merely nodded his head and opened a very heavy gate near the vehicle entrance. The tall man made a swift pattern over the Rabbi's person with a metal detector and then pointed at the retinal scanner.

There was a click, and the door lock released. Oddly, the tall man opened the door and actually cracked a small smile for an instant. The Rabbi entered the main foyer. Two receptionists smiled nicely and one pointed toward a partially opened door. He walked stiffly over and entered the room.

Again, no one was in the room other than he. The straight-backed chair looked less than inviting, but he sat and began to wait. One of the receptionists startled him by closing the door to the foyer. He could hear the lock mechanism drive the large bolt into the metal frame.

He thumbed a small circle of beads he carried in his pocket; he used these as a stress reliever, much more often now as he was attempting to quit smoking. As before, the only other door into the room opened, and in walked the woman he had spoken to previously. She was instantly recognizable, as scarring disturbed the upper right side of her face.

"Well, Rabbi, thank you for coming to chat." She smiled a lop-sided smile owing to the depth of the scarring into her facial muscles. "I hope you are well."

"Yes, I am well." Right at the moment his stomach was in knots and his right index finger and middle finger curled around an imaginary cigarette.

"And how are your efforts to stop smoking, Rabbi?" she asked.

He sat upright at the question. The Rabbi went to great pains to hide his smoking from the public. "How?" The

Rabbi's mouth gaped opened and closed several times, "How did you know?"

Mrs. Smith gave him the same lop-sided smile, "Sir, we know everything." He started to ask another question but was silenced with a wave of her hand.

"Forgive us, Rabbi, you would not have gotten here had we not known everything about you." She frowned and looked at the electronic desk top, "Just like we know everything about your brother."

The Rabbi flushed an angry red, starting from his neck and working up across his face. "What do you know about my brother? And I resent the--" he stopped, waved to silence with another gesture.

"We know." She looked up from the desk top. "I have a question to ask of you."

For the first time to his knowledge, she stood, walked over to him, and placed a hand upon his shoulder. "It is a very important question."

108

---

Adiba did her research on Kadar, and found trails leading nowhere at every turn. She became intrigued with the handsome man who was smart and pleasant.

An off-hand comment from a family friend at a 70th birthday party for a patriarch of the Arabic community in Milwaukee caught her ear. As quickly as the words were spoken, the man became nervous and fairly shouted, "As if any of that could be true!" for all to hear. Still, what she heard about the mysterious Kadar made her re-double her efforts to dig deeper.

## 109

Kadar reloaded the 9mm quickly and commenced to throwing lead down range at the target. His friend shouted, "Reload!" into his ear. Expertly Kadar dropped the magazine and pulled a full one from his belt. The spent dropped magazine had not stopped rattling on the table in front of him when he was able to send more bullets down range. The slide stayed open when the last shell casing was ejected. A hand slapped him on the shoulder, "Great job, Wyatt Earp!"

Kadar looked to the left and right ascertaining that he and his companion were still the only shooters in the 25-yard range, "Yes, practice does help." He placed the gun on the table and smiled. "I think it is time that we all spent more time here." His companion used the target-retrieval mechanism. The John Dillinger target silhouette stopped and flapped a little until it came to a rest. Under the target Kadar had scribbled "Neah Bey."

His last communication from Mrs. T gave him details on Fahd, Astoria, and this mysterious Neah Bey. His companion taped over the holes Kadar had blown into the target and sent it back down the range. The money they used for all such purposes came from their own pockets and had to be used wisely. Kadar smiled; his companion was very skilled and filled the ten spot with holes. Pity it was just a paper target and not really the nefarious Neah Bey. Or, his smile deepened, that arrogant Rahman impersonator, Fahd.

## 110

Mrs. T scanned her emails; nothing really important jumped from the computer-backed eye-ware. She sat in the Starbucks down on First Avenue, just a few blocks from the football and baseball stadiums. The latte was nice and hot; the biscotti she nibbled at was lifeless and devoid of flavor. She made far better ones herself using a custom biscotti pan she found online. The selected email messages played through her computer glasses. They were very secure.

## 111

The future Mrs. T was simply known as T as a child. She added the "Mrs." to ward off unwanted advances from her male counterparts.

It seemed like an age ago when she ran for cover as a child in Herzegovina. Concrete chips showered down on her as the heavy bullets slapped into what was left of the school. The sectarian violence had already claimed most of her family, then the barn, outbuildings, and finally the house. She cried when the roof fell in, sending a roiling plume of fire and sparks into the cold night sky. Her brother helped her cross the valley and out of her homeland.

It took nearly a week for the two children to hike to Sarajevo. Metok provided for them by stealing food from farms. He was slender and could run like the wind, a valuable skill when it came time to grab a loaf of bread and run for it. All they had was a scrap of paper with a family name and the name of a street. It was difficult for the children, as they were Muslims in a Christian world. Their distant relatives were apprehensive about taking them in at all. Finally, the wife forced the husband into letting the children stay, at least for a little bit.

The husband, a brutish man with few skills, worked as a bricklayer. One concession he forced from his wife that if the children stayed, they would look, act, and worship like Christians. On this he was unyielding. It would be camouflage and provide protection for the children as well as for the man and woman.

The children practiced English daily, and gave up their traditional garb. In quiet moments, Metok would read from his copy of the Koran, which he kept hidden from their stepparents.

T was fascinated by the imagery that Metok could weave through her mind with mere words. In private they prayed as often as they could.

Life was disconnected. They knew that the life before was over and they had to fit in here, but here was not home, and never would be.

After ten years, Metok contracted the flu and died with T by his side. The American peacekeeping mission refused to fly him to a hospital, refused to allow a doctor to travel the roads, and delayed getting the medicine in time. Yet they could crisscross the sky with jet aircraft, awaken them with the roar of CH-53 Marine helicopters in the early hours, and rumble through the streets in armored convoys. Metok burned up from a fever in a pile of dirty blankets that was the bed they shared.

T cursed the Americans. Two years later, after doing her chores and the ones unfilled by Metok, her stepmother died. Within a fortnight, her stepfather…

## 112

The Rabbi returned to the Smith, LLC, one week later. Again the ritual of being wanded by the tall man, again the trepidation walking through the foyer, again the hard wood chair, and again the wait.

This time within a second of his sitting down, the other door opened. The woman with the scarred face entered the room.

"Thank you for coming back, Rabbi." Again the lop-sided smile, however brief. "And what have you to tell me?"

The Rabbi leaned forward. "It is a difficult question you have asked." He bit his lower lip and glanced around the room. "We have come and gone? Is that it? We started over?"

"That is what the data and artifacts indicate." No smile, no frown, no emotion tainted her comment.

He placed his hands on his face, hiding the fear and nausea that swept over him. "All I can tell you, if this is true--and how could it be--this would crush our sometimes tenuous hold on our beliefs." Sitting back, he waited for an answer.

"Why would you say 'tenuous hold' Rabbi?" she asked.

"God created the heavens and the earth; He created night and day, the oceans and the firmament." The Rabbi stopped. "Nowhere does it say he did it *twice*."

She studied the desk top. "Rabbi, we are not talking about the earth itself, we are talking about the human race."

"The point is the same, just how many Adams and Eves do you remember there being in the Old Testament?" He thumbed the beads quickly in his pocket. In retracing his

150

steps from the synagogue to the Smith house he counted no less than five convenience stores where he could buy a pack of Marlboros. "A study of the story of Noah actually supports this; there was still just one Adam, and just one Eve. The Book of Genesis states rather emphatically: 'God formed a man from dust and breathed life into him.' I do not add to the quotation. It is the Word of God that describes 'man' and not 'men.' The same is reflected in the creation of Eve, as a singular woman. We are all descendants of them."

"Very well, Rabbi." She looked up, the sunlight streaming in through the extraordinarily thick glass highlighting the scars on her face. He squinted at the image. Briefly her hand covered the right side of her face.

"I'm sorry, I have been rude." He looked down in embarrassment.

"Not to worry, I consider it a badge of honor." Her eyes burned a hole into his discomfort. "But let us ask the difficult question," her gaze did not falter. "What will happen?"

The Rabbi cleared his throat, "We, as the human race are the most incredibly powerful force in the universe. And yet, as individuals, we can sometimes be so frail." Tears welled up in his eyes. "My fear, my deepest fear, is that we will throw off the collective good and become frail, vulnerable, and flawed human individuals." With his hand he cleared the tears from his face, "And most certainly my people can attest to that."

He looked up and saw the lower lip of Ms. Smith tremble. She simply nodded toward the door; the interview was over. As he exited the front door, the tall man handed him an envelope.

"Per our agreement, sir." The tall man motioned for another guard to walk the Rabbi to the gate.

He made it past the first three convenience stores, but not the fourth.

## 113

Adiba was not one to shy away from hard work when something needed to be dug out; indeed, she was sent to Montana for help with the discovery and rescue of a nearly complete Tyrannosaurus Rex skeleton buried under a sacred place for the Native Americans. Possibly her looks, the jet black hair, the olive complexion, and her penchant for wearing garb similar to the Kootenai of Northwest Montana made her the favorite of the local Chiefs.

Expeditions to Mongolia, the Amazon, and the North Slope of Alaska followed. She was tough physically and mentally.

She profaned the traditional degraded stature of women in the Arabic world, and that was on her mind when she barged into a meeting Kadar was having in Mount Carroll, Illinois.

The three men stood, outraged that their supposedly private conversation was interrupted by this woman. Kadar rose to his six feet-two inches and shouted, "How dare you!"

Adiba smirked and said "Fools! If I found you this easily, what problem would it be for the CIA or the NSA?" She stepped forward, chin thrust out, a snarl on her lips, knowing that this would be considered the ultimate transgression for a woman.

Kadar was not going to be challenged in such a manner in front of his associates; such an affront must be dealt with quickly and decisively. He raised his arm to backhand the woman to her knees and stepped forward.

Adiba shrieked and spun to her right feigning mortal fear. Kadar hesitated ever so briefly, and that was his undoing.

As she spun to her right she whipped out the collapsible baton used by police agencies everywhere. Adiba had done her watching with great care; Kadar was left-handed. As he tried to correct for the blow, the truncheon caught him on the right side of the head and drove him to his knees.

From his knees Kadar shouted, "Kill the bitch!" He was stunned to see that his compatriots stood motionless next to him. "I said, kill the--" again pain washed over his head as the baton struck again. From the floor Kadar looked up to see Adiba pointing a short-barreled but large caliber hand gun at the groin of the nearest man.

"Want a new name? Like Dick-less?" Adiba pulled the hammer back to emphasis the point.

The two standing men took one large step backwards each. Adiba motioned to them to sit together on the couch. They complied. Shocked, Kadar looked up into the face of Adiba. He rose to the kneeling position. Holding the baton in one hand she ground the muzzle of the revolver into Kadar's forehead. "I will be treated as an equal, or you will die, right here, right now. Make up your mind. Five. Four. Three."

Kadar bowed his head, the ultimate posture of subjugation. "You are equal."

Adiba pulled the gun away and motioned to Kadar to take a seat next to his associates. "Now that we have the introductions out of the way, I suggest we figure out how to develop a winning strategy, don't you agree? And possibly do much better on security, right?" It seemed to the seated men that as contrary opinions might produce lethal results, they all nodded in agreement.

When they were finished talking, Adiba cocked the revolver and pointed it at each man's head. "I think we can all rest easier if we conduct our affairs remotely going forward." She rose and slowly backed from the room.

## 114

The Rabbi set the phone back on the desk. It was from the Smiths, the woman with the scarred face in fact. She had asked if he was going to be in the office on the following day around ten-thirty a.m.

It was now ten thirty-five, and he waited for the phone to ring. Instead, there was a knock on the door. The knock surprised him, as he was entirely focused on the phone.

"Yes! Yes! Come in." He shouted impatiently. The door swung open and in walked his brother. He was thin, bruised, and looked exhausted. Stubble of beard circled the lower part of his face. There were bandages on his neck and both hands. His Israeli uniform was tattered and bloody; the Rabbi could see the perspiration stains from across the room.

The Rabbi leapt to his feet and ran to his brother, "Moshe! Moshe! How is this possible?" They embraced.

"Brother! I am so very tired." And with that Moshe sat down. "I do not know. I was captured, and they told me I was going to be set on fire and filmed." Moshe shook his head from side to side in disbelief. The Rabbi dragged a chair over and sat next to his brother.

"But how? We had given up hope!" The Rabbi smiled and grabbed his brother's hand and shook it repeatedly.

"I was sitting in my cage; there were explosions all around. Machine guns fired all along the perimeter." He put his hand on his brother's shoulder, "People came running into the room, many explosions, grenades, and I could hear a helicopter overhead.

"Then it was very strange. A man as old as Dad came in, bleeding from a shoulder wound and a woman beside him." His mouth opened and closed several times. "The man and the woman were, were, what is the term? Demons, ghosts, what is the old word?"

The Rabbi thought for a moment and said, "Like *Dybbuk*?"

Moshe shouted, "Yes! They were *Dybbuk*! They fought and shot everyone. The woman used a small machine gun and a knife; the old man used an old 1911 .45 pistol." The Rabbi had no idea what a 1911 .45 was but assumed that it was a formidable weapon of some sort.

"They got me out of the cage and took me by the arms and led me from the room into the night." Moshe stared around the room thinking of his next words.

"There were bodies everywhere, and the old man and woman had friends. Many friends." Moshe swallowed, "They killed everyone. I mean everyone!" He paused to gather his thoughts.

"They had a helicopter and threw me in it. The attackers jumped in and continued to shoot everywhere, everything, and everyone. I have never seen such a thing!" Moshe grasped his brother's hands and held them.

"What happened? What did they say?" The Rabbi asked.

"Nothing! The woman that sat next to me finally said,

'Here, this will help.' She gave me a shot and I passed out."
He squeezed his hands around the Rabbi's. "I woke up on
a United States aircraft carrier and was ordered to get into
a jet that was launched right away."

Moshe shook his head repeatedly. "We were re-fueled
in midair several times, and landed about fifteen kilometers from here. They gave me this to give to you." Moshe
took a small envelope from his breast pocket and handed
it unopened to the Rabbi.

"What is this?" The older brother turned the envelope
over and over in his hands.

Moshe smiled, "Well, from here brother, it looks like
an envelope."

"Yes, it does." The Rabbi looked at his brash brother,
frowning, "Yes, I rather figured that out myself."

He tore open the envelope and extracted one half of
a three by five note card. Handwritten were the words,
"You are welcome, Ms. S." The Rabbi sat back and saw
writing on the back of the card, "Job 1.21" He looked at
his brother that had just been snatched from death, and
realized his position. *"The Lord has given, and the Lord has
taken away."* The Rabbi understood the message. The
Smiths had given him his brother and could just as easily
take him away.

"What does that mean? It's a passage, isn't it?" Moshe
reached for the paper, but the Rabbi folded it up and put
it in a pocket.

"How about we celebrate someplace nice tonight?"
the Rabbi asked.

156

## 115

The things Astoria had taken from the ice shelf were split into two groups. The ones he felt proved his point adequately and those that were perfect. Perfect in the sense that he had surreptitiously conducted carbon dating on them. He also challenged some of his brighter students to conduct an analysis on the samples. Astoria played a game with some of his doctoral candidates; break down the small sample and tell him what it was.

He stated that he had contacts in DARPA and at NASA that had sent him special samples of new alloys to be used in spacecraft of the future. The students accepted the challenge. The results were surprising. The metal fragments were peculiar alloys of nickel and stainless steel, but were millions of years old, possibly billions. The students concluded that the world had been scoured for exotic meteorites that were used in the metal parts. Dr. Dayton Astoria made sure the small fragments that he gave his three select students did not have the intricate language carved into them.

## 116

Kadar spoke with Adiba. He had been summoned to a chat room with that witch Mrs. T. For now, anyway, he would endure her haughty indifference. Apparently through the research of Rahman, the location of artifacts had been secured in the Smithsonian. The fates were kind to them in providing an insider to help at such a critical moment. Adiba knew the location of the room in question, and she had access to the area through her security passes. It would be an easy task to accomplish.

No one would question the intern as she drifted from one forlorn pile of antiquities to another in a sub-basement of an offsite warehouse. Still, it perplexed her some to find on the log sheet that Dr. Astoria had been in the area just hours before. No matter, the bookish professor was not on her radar. She found the room and peeked inside. It was a smallish room set apart from the rest. Her glance told her the labels on the shelves were at least sixty years old or more. Everything seemed in order, and she would return in a few days to delve into the contents.

## 117

Neah stared across the kitchen island at Dr. Dayton Astoria. Ravenna Lakota knew where Ione put the battle pack, and from that she withdrew the first aid kit. Astoria nearly bolted for the door when he saw Ravenna pull out the syringe of numbing agent.

Ione placed a hand on his forearm and said, "She has stitched up Neah on many occasions, so don't worry, Doctor, she knows her stuff." Astoria calmed down and let Ravenna tend to his injuries. In a few minutes she had numbed a spot on Astoria's shoulder and placed three stitches in a wound.

By that time Ione had brought out some grey gym gear. "Here, the shower is right over there in the guest bathroom. You'll find everything you need in there."

Astoria's eyes rolled around the room at Ravenna, Ione,

and Neah. "I know you saved my life, but are you just being nice before you kill me, or what?" Neah smiled.

Ravenna spoke forcefully, "Doctor, shower, change your clothes, and we'll have a snack ready for you. What kind of beverage would you like?"

Astoria stepped toward the shower, "Beverage? Like soda pop or something?"

Ione pulled open the pantry door revealing the built-in wine cooler and the ample supply of other liquids. "Well, if that's what you prefer, fine, but we have a collection of more adult offerings." She reached for the GlenDronach 21.

He smiled, "That is an excellent choice." Ravenna dug out a glass, and motioned toward an ice bucket. Astoria waved the ice off.

Ione handed him the bottle, "See you when you get out of the shower. What would you like to have as a snack?"

With the gym clothes over one shoulder, a glass in one hand, and a twenty-one-year-old bottle of Scotch in the other he shrugged. "Whatever is easiest?"

### 118

Neah waited at the entrance to the gated area of the convent. A short picket fence enclosed the main house. He could have stepped over it with no trouble. The early snow in this part of Montana whipped small flakes around his legs, making him glad he wore some thin but effective long underwear. It took a while, but eventually a member of the Order saw him and opened the front door.

She did not beckon him closer, and indeed she raised a flat palm toward him to keep him in his place. Her thin clothes and her complete emotionless countenance in the face of an icy breeze bespoke a hidden inner strength.

The Sister stopped six feet away and simply stared into Neah Bey's eyes.

"Hello?" Neah waited for a response, there was none.

"I am an old friend of Silesia. May I speak to her?" The cold was beginning to make Bey shiver.

The Sister spoke, "We have no one here with that name."

"I, well, I" Bey floundered, "Look, that was her name when I knew her, not the name she may have taken here."

Her eyes narrowed for a moment, and then she turned and walked back to the door. She turned and again raised the palm towards him.

The cold was seeping through his shoes and into his feet.

### 119

Adiba walked past Security Officer Copalis and smiled. She liked the old retired Washington, D.C., cop. "Hello, Sergeant! How are you today?"

Copalis looked up from behind the guard station, frown lines showing at the corners of his eyes and mouth. "Well, dang this technology! All the cameras from the loading dock to the basement are down. Nothing but old-time TV snow!" He pointed at the buzzy white and black screens. "See? Nothing working at all. Had to call the tech dimwits from downtown. They are stuck in traffic and won't be here for a month of Sundays, if they do come at all."

She peered over the burly man's shoulders and patted his back. "There, there, Sar-gee, every little thing will work out just fine. Can I borrow a flashlight if it is a power failure down there in the tomb?"

Copalis calmed down, "Sure, but I can lock the door and walk down with you, if you like, you know, big scary spiders and rats the size of Volkswagen vans and all."

Adiba laughed, "No, I'll be fine!"

The old cop laughed, "Heck, I know that, I was worried for me! Here, take the spare radio and give a shout if something is wonky."

She stuffed the radio in her carry bag and tucked the flashlight under her arm. "No worries! I'll shout if I see anything." Adiba walked across the main floor to the stairwell that backed up against the loading dock on the main level. Her badge swiped across the card reader and unlocked the door to the stairs leading to the lower levels. The lights were on in the stairs, and she could see lights through the wire glass on the lower level. "Lights are on down here, Sar-gee!"

He laughed into the radio, "Thanks, young lady! Be careful." She opened the door and walked across the floor to the Antarctica Storage Room C-124. The door was ajar. Her foot pushed it open, and she reached for the light switch. The room, its contents, even the shelving were gone. It appeared that the floor had been swept. She turned back toward the stairs and noticed the closed-circuit television camera was covered in black garbage sacks and was swinging slightly from its disconnected cable and power cord. "Sergeant! Sergeant! We've been robbed!" Adiba shouted into the radio, twice. The first time in her excitement she forgot to key the mic.

In spite of his age and bad hip, retired Washington, D.C., Sergeant Ridgefield Copalis made it to the basement in record time. He took one look in the room and at the camera. From his holster he pulled out his Smith and Wesson Model 10 .357 Magnum, and with his other hand pulled Adiba behind him to protect her. In a few minutes they were outside, the Sergeant barking commands into his radio and cellphone simultaneously. Sirens wailed in the distance, the cops always driving a little faster when one of their own was beckoning them.

## 120

Ravenna Lakota could pass for Hispanic, Native American, Arabic, and Italian. In fact, she had done just that on several occasions. She knew many people all over the world, but had few friends. Ravenna stopped the highly customized Kawasaki Ninja, which boasted of nearly one thousand ccs of supercharged muscle, and removed her helmet. The leather pants and jacket were form-fitting and did an excellent job of highlighting her muscular, yet shapely figure. The helmet was placed on the seat of the big machine.

It was a small house, nothing noteworthy at all, located east, outside of Flagstaff, Arizona. She knocked on the door frame.

Shuffling footsteps could be heard, and the door opened. The darkened interior and the bright exterior sunlight made visualizing the figure inside difficult.

A soft voice said, "Welcome home, little one, the Salt House Clan welcomes you." She stepped in and closed the door behind her.

"I am glad that you are home so we could chat," Ravenna said.

The elderly figure sat on a handmade chair of thin slats of wood and what may have been deer hide. "These old bones are not much for traveling these days." In the dim light the glint of a smile could be seen. "But then I have traveled further than most."

Ravenna sat on a small rug in the center of the room, "That is very true; you are one of the last of the Wind Talkers."

"Ah, a lifetime ago, and half a world away." Again the soft smile. "I prefer to spend my time in the reverence of the planet and trying to teach the younger ones our language."

There was a brief silence in the room. Ravenna inhaled to speak but was cut off by the elderly man.

"You did not come here to listen to me; you came here so I could listen to you." A crow cawed loudly from the peak of the house. The old man listed his head to one side, as if trying to discern the language of the crow. "Well, my friend is summoning the spirits to open their arms for me."

Ravenna asked of her uncle, "What do the legends say about the human race coming to the planet's surface, and nearly dying out, and then returning?"

"Well, that is a very good question. Did you try Googling for an answer?" The soft laughter of the old man filled the room with a magical sound. Ravenna covered her mouth in embarrassment.

"Uncle, if it were as simple as that..." Her voice trailed off.

"I know, nothing is ever that simple anymore, is it?" He took a breath, "I sense urgency in your voice. Tell me everything." The crow took up his raucous calling. "And possibly in as short as time as possible."

## 121

She sat back and stared at the remains of the heist. The Trade Group liaison was more than upset. Her foot kicked a nearly century old Antarctic artifact across the floor. "God damn that Astoria! He shoplifted it! If you can't trust a milquetoast, pencil-necked, four-eyed *academician,* then who the hell can you trust?" The Trade Group would not be pleased to hear that there had been an end-run by a small town university geek. They had planned the robbery of the Smithsonian for months. She grabbed a dossier of Astoria and stabbed it with a pencil. "Rot in hell, teacher!"

## 122

Astoria rubbed himself down with the thick Turkish towel. He found all the usual amenities for him. There was a small basket set on the vanity countertop, a fine collection of high-grade toiletries. Astoria slipped into the gym clothes and opened the door to the main room. His belly was warmed slightly by the excellent Scotch. He felt relieved that the guns were out of sight. Ione smiled and motioned him to a high-backed bar stool that had been moved into the kitchen area. Spread out on the other side of the kitchen was a spread of sandwich makings and two kinds of soup.

Neah Bey sat at the end of the table deep in conversation with Ravenna Lakota; they were peering over maps of the Antarctic. Ione was holding a large animated cat that had what appeared to be a horsetail waving about.

It looked something like a Siamese but with a much wilder countenance.

Underfoot another cat looked like the Phantom of the Opera with his white masked face rubbing up against Ione's legs and then a chair leg. The smell of the warm soup filled the air. It seemed like the nearest thing to home Dr. Dayton Astoria had been in for more than a decade. Ione helped him make a sandwich and poured him a bowl of steaming vegetable beef soup. Not the canned stuff, but homemade, the vegetables large and not cooked into mush. As he sampled the soup to test its temperature, he felt he was being watched. Across the room Euripides the Wonder Cat was ensconced in a custom carpet-lined stand. The big cat yawned, displaying an impressive set of teeth.

When he settled in and had a few bites of the sandwich and several spoons of soup, Neah Bey looked up from the map and asked, "Where is it?"

123

---

They were partners on a mission, he and Tieton. It had ended very badly. There was a running gun battle through Monterrey, Mexico. The bad guys outnumbered the good guys. And the bad guys did not have any hesitation in shooting at Tieton and Neah on crowded streets. Civilians ran in all directions; some lay silent in pools of their own blood.

Less than one hundred yards before they would fall under the protective umbrella of a covert Marine Corp rifle company, a heavy machine gun disguised in an ice cream truck opened up. Parts of the little car flew off in all directions. Sparks appeared and disappeared as heavy bullets flew thru the thin metal skin of the car.

The engine stuttered and stopped, but mercifully it was inside the fire zone of the Marines. Accurate return fire erupted from roof tops, alleys, and doorways. The bad guys fell dead or retreated.

Bey was holding his left bicep with his right hand. He turned toward Tieton.

"Let's get out of this car and..." Bey grew silent. Tieton was dead, three holes across his chest from the machine gun oozed blood.

Marines descended on the car, literally ripping the doors off the hinges with their bare hands. Corpsmen began attending them, until it was clear that Tieton had not survived. A half dozen took up kneeling positions to either side of the wreck and defended the others.

Bey had the duty of telling Tieton's wife, Silesia, of his death in the line of duty in a foreign country. She collapsed in the doorway and had a miscarriage of Tieton's child.

Neah and Ione called frequently for a few months thereafter, and then the number of times Silesia answered began to reduce, until finally all they could do was leave phone messages and emails that were never returned.

Neah sent a local unit over to see if everything was okay. He found out that Silesia had sold all her possessions and her home. She fell off the radar. Neah put a trace on all her credit cards, cell phone, anything that would help him track her down.

He got a hit on a credit card in Montana and was able to track her cell phone to the convent. Every anniversary thereafter, Ione and Neah would send an anonymous check to the convent in the memory of Tieton.

## 124

Bey now stood slowly freezing to death at the gate to the cloister where Silesia now called home. Slowly the door opened and Silesia appeared, a small thin shawl wrapped her shoulders. She pulled the shawl a little closer.

Neah smiled. Silesia did not. She walked to within six feet of Neah and stopped.

"Hello, Sil." Neah began to shiver.

"I know you tried, Neah." She spoke slowly. "I read the reports the Smiths would let me see."

Neah looked down to the snowflakes whispering around his legs. "He didn't suffer, Sil."

"I know, Neah. Was it worth it?" She asked.

"Do you mean was it worth losing Tieton over? No, no it was not." Neah continued to study the snowflakes. "I, I, well, I have relived that day a thousand times." He pushed a little skiff of snow into a mound and then stepped on it.

"Me, too." Sil stepped closer, and Neah looked up. She took her thin cold hand and placed it alongside Neah's face. "You were Tieton's best friend."

Neah took his hand and held it over hers, pressing it closer into his face. "I miss him so much." He choked back the wave of sorrow that engulfed him.

She let her hand warm against Neah's face for a moment longer.

"Well, aren't we a pair?" she said as she withdrew her hand. "I am guessing you came here for something to do with work?"

Neah longed for the return of her hand to his face. He

shook it off and said, "You always knew when to ask the big questions, Sil."

"Come in out of the cold." She turned towards the door. There were faces of other Sisters near the windows, watching them.

Neah took a half step forward then stopped. "Are you sure? Is this okay?"

Silesia quietly laughed. "Yes, Neah. I assure you that you will be safe from the Sisters."

Neah Bey turned crimson and flustered but followed in some measure of reluctance.

## 125

Kadar shouted at Adiba, "You do not have it? Where is it? How could you let it get away?"

Adiba remained silent for a moment. "If I had a time frame, that would have helped. If I had an idea of the importance, that would have helped. So get off your high horse. You kept information from me. Deal with it."

Kadar took a deep breath preparing to shout. It took considerable effort to remain civil. "Okay!! Okay! Okay." It took strength to lower his volume and his tone. "I'm very concerned too. All I know, all that I think I know, is that we should suspect Neah Bey and associates first, and all others second." He took another deep breath. "Are you with us?"

Adiba spoke clearly and concisely, "Yes, I am."

## 126

Ravenna hugged her uncle and said, "Thank you for explaining it to me." She lingered her hand on the old man's shoulder. "I am not sure I understand it all."

The old man sat heavily back into the chair, "We are the strongest, as any people would be, when we are together and the weakest when we are not. What you have suggested will break us into little pieces. We may not have the strength to gather ourselves."

The crow called again. "Someone seems impatient."

Ravenna hugged her uncle again, and said, "Thank you." And with that, she left. She had arrived at ten in the morning and realized that it was now noon of the following day.

At a truck stop in southern Utah she phoned Neah.

## 127

She endured much at the hands of her stepfather, some things she tried to burn from her brain with drugs and alcohol. One night while she was trying to sneak some of her tormentor's vodka, he struck her from behind. It was a stunning blow that sent her flying across the room. He grabbed at her skirt, as he had done before. She fought back, striking him with her fists and nails.

He roared in drunken laughter, "You think you can hurt me?" His breath stank of cigarettes and cheap liquor. He backhanded her again and again. Blood flowed from her nose and split lip. She cried out and fell heavily against the roughhewn table knocking the dishes and cutlery to the floor. He grabbed at her undergarments, pulling them to her knees.

She struck out with all that she had access to, a large fork from a carving set which they used to slice the slabs of meat they bought or stole. Had he left the fork in his neck, he might have lived. By pulling it out he left open the hole the tine made in his carotid artery. A stream of blood shot across the room until his hand clamped on his neck. He looked wildly about, a cloth, a towel, her ruined dress, anything to stop the blood loss. His vision tunneled down. He staggered across the floor, her torn dress held against his neck. His hearing began to fail. Strange circles of darkness appeared at the periphery of his vision.

In his chest his heart began to commit cyclical failures, skipping beats, beating quickly, stopping briefly and then racing. A dull ache began at his core and spread outward. His last sight was of his stepdaughter, half naked, blood trails from her lip and nose, taking the other half of the carving set, a long thick heavy stag-horned handled blade which she began stabbing into his chest.

## 128

Dr. Dayton Astoria prohibited anyone from being near the deceased Madison. With as much tenderness as he could muster, he pulled the frozen corpse--no, not just a corpse, a friend--to the supply tent. He had ordered the temperature to be raised as high as possible so that, well, so that his friend would thaw a little. Astoria stayed with Madison's remains for two days until he became pliable enough to bend into a position that he could stuff into a sleeping bag.

Astoria kept his word and stayed with Madison's remains until they hit their port of entry into the United States. Out of his own pocket he rented a hearse and accompanied the simple casket all the way to the remote corner of Washington State.

Madison's mother was too distraught to make any arrangements, so Astoria exchanged a dozen cell phone calls with Albion, the brother. It was going to be a simple ceremony attended by fewer than a dozen colleagues from school and from the ice.

At the service Astoria spoke briefly about the research that Madison was involved in and what that would mean to further humankind's knowledge of the earth. He was the last person to see the remains of his student. Astoria placed both hands on the lip of the open casket, let slip into the opening a small remembrance, and then personally closed and locked the lid. Madison's mother fainted and was attended by her surviving son. Pierce, Astoria, a pair of high school friends, and two fellow researchers carried the casket out of the mortuary in Colville and into the hearse. From there it was an hour drive to the Metaline Cemetery where Madison would be laid to rest next to his father, who had passed away when Madison was very young.

Astoria maintained his composure until one of Madison's high school friends told him of a conversation that took place when Madison was home last. The young man told him that Madison was fascinated with the ice, but afraid of the dangers until he worked with Dr. Astoria. He related that Madison would only go back on expeditions with Astoria, as he was the only one he had faith in. Pierce put an arm around Astoria and led him to the car. They got very drunk on the ride back to Ellensburg.

It took half a day for Astoria to walk around the campus to find his car, parked halfway on the street, and the other half in a flower garden pointed the wrong way on a one-way street. A look in the back seat revealed a snoring Pierce using a pizza box as a pillow. How the massive Pierce had stuffed himself in the back seat was a mystery.

## 129

Silesia opened the door to the small office and waved Neah in. There was a small wooden table with two straight-backed chairs with no cushions. It was scarcely any warmer inside than outside. An ancient laptop was cabled over to an equally ancient dot matrix printer that still used the paper with the perforated edges.

Neah sat after Silesia. The door was left partially open. An occasional figure passed by.

He cranked his neck around and looked at the open door. Silesia saw his discomfort and said, "The door stays open, Neah. It's just the way things are." She smiled as his discomfort grew. "Don't worry, Neah, we are all in our own world here. What gets said here will not be heard by anyone who will care."

Neah surrendered and slumped back in the chair. "Well, of all the people on the planet, I have always trusted you at the same level as Ione and Ravenna."

Silesia smiled, "How is Ione? And Ravenna? Is Ravenna the same beautiful but deadly creature that I remember?"

"Ione is fine, she has to deal with three cats, Euripides, Socrates, and Mr. Morley. Her quilting expertise has grown, and I have asked her many times to enter her quilts in various fairs and shows." He shook his head slightly side to side. "Ravenna is still beautiful, and still deadly. She has saved me..." He winced at treading on the subject of why he was alive and Tieton dead.

"Don't worry, Neah!" Silesia's face shadowed briefly, "I have come to accept the situation, and I hope you have too."

Neah looked down and studied the wooden floor, clean, but much worn. "I never will." To himself he said, *and there are still a few to track down who killed your husband, and I will do just that. That is a promise.*

"Well, enough of old times good and bad, what do you want?" Silesia leaned forward and placed a hand on Neah's knee.

"I need a feeling, a sense of direction, a view of what might happen if something specific happened." Neah's eyes traced around the room; it needed painting. Only two of the three light bulbs in the room worked.

The pressure on his knee increased. "Tell me," she directed.

130

---

Mrs. T sat back from the laptop. A picture of Neah Bey faded as the computer went to sleep. She had exchanged emails with Kadar, Adiba, and Fahd. They set a date to meet in Seattle. She opened her desk drawer and used her favorite knife to open her mail. The stag horn was well worn. "Well, old friend, haven't we had a time of it? I may need your services again." She expertly flipped the knife in her hands. Her eyes scanned over the printed email and focused on Fahd's name. "And yet again."

### 131

Fahd waited patiently for the line to shrink down. He paid for the ferry ride with cash as a walk-on.

### 132

Kadar kept the Road King down to a dull roar when he steered it onto the Super-Class Ferry Yakima. Motorcycles were always pushed to the front of the line, first on and first off.

### 133

Mrs. T paid for the cab to take her to the ferry leaving the Colman Dock in downtown Seattle.

### 134

Astoria looked from Ione who was still smiling and holding an immense yet fidgety cat, to the others. Ravenna's face was expressionless; it was like looking at a face carved in ice. Neah Bey sat with hands hidden under the lip of the counter top.

Astoria sat down, his head hung against his chest. "If I tell you, I die? Right?"

Neah tilted his head to one side. "Not really what we want to do, Doctor. We would rather you became part of the team." His hands still were hidden by the counter top. Ravenna Lakota, like smoke in the trees, slipped further to the doctor's left, splitting the doctor's focus. Now her hands were below the counter top. The only hands other than his own that he could see were Ione Bey's. He looked to her and asked, "What do I do?" His voice cracked a little.

Ione stopped smiling and let the large cat drop to the floor. "I would listen to them and do as they ask. I assure you that whatever they decide will be true. Hopefully your words will mean they protect you. In that case, you will have no fears." She frowned, "They can be prone to the use of force in dramatic ways, of that I assure you." Her eyes traced over the almost concealed fracture of where part of her house was knocked down and then rebuilt. Through the window she could see the new brickwork on the patio where the RPG landed. She placed a hand on Dr. Astoria's shoulder, "They will protect you better than anyone else on the planet. Trust them."

Astoria nodded, "I understand." He sighed and told them the story of the extra contents of Madison's casket, safely buried in the small Eastern Washington town of Metaline Falls.

Neah looked at Ravenna and said, "Well, that will be a first."

Ione did not understand, "First for what?"

Ravenna answered simply, "Grave robbery."

Astoria looked glumly out the window. It started to rain.

175

## 135

They arrived at the stern observation deck, looking southeast toward Mount Rainier as the Yakima drove through whitecaps to Bremerton. The exhaust for the massive stack drifted to this part of the ferry, making company from other passengers less likely. Kadar fumbled with a camera and pretended to take pictures. "Well, here we are; the means to an end."

Mrs. T said nothing. Fahd looked out of the corners of his eyes, left to the woman and right to Kadar. "No, we are the means to a beginning." Fahd did not like being between Kadar and the woman T. Purposefully he wandered around the rain-slicked deck to put Kadar between himself and her.

Mrs. T laughed at both of them, "All of those things are minor! It has always been about the money and the power. Don't lose sight of that. Those are the two things that drive the universe. If the other stuff is what makes your dreams come true, then fine."

Fahd and Kadar were silent for a moment, and then acquiesced. "That is the truth within the truth," Fahd said, and Kadar nodded his head in agreement.

Mrs. T slowly took her hand off the shrouded hammer .38 Special snub-nosed revolver. Possibly these two pawns had a use.

## 136

It was a lonely ride back to Southwest Washington from Montana. Neah had much to ponder. In the end Silesia had risen and left the room, returning with the elderly Sister who had confronted Bey at the gate. Silesia looked at Neah and said, "Repeat what you have told me." She knelt by the elderly woman. "Sister, you are going to hear things that are very important to this man, who is a friend of mine from long ago."

The petit woman pierced Neah with her gaze and said, "Proceed." Her eyes were bottomless pools of darkness into which Neah felt trapped.

As he wove his story, the old woman would nod her head, lean forward to listen intently, and then settle back, always the eyes staring into his. In spite of the chill to the room, sweat began to trace down Neah's chest and back.

The brief statement she made in closure had nearly stopped his heart. He stepped a little more forcefully on the accelerator to put as much distance between him and the old woman.

Upon his arrival back home, Ravenna and Ione were in the kitchen, two empty bottles of wine on the kitchen counter. Ravenna indicated that Astoria was in the guest bedroom resting

Ravenna said, "If your conversation with Silesia was anything like the one I had with my uncle, you'd have a drink or two yourself." Neah looked around and shook his head.

"No, that isn't going to help." Neah's shoulders slumped with fatigue.

Ione asked, "How is Silesia?"

"She is fine, asked about you two, wanted to know what you were doing." Neah sat down, and Mr. Morley rubbed up against his leg.

Ione got up, "Let me get something for us to snack on."

Ravenna's eyes followed Ione out of the room, and looked back to match eyes with Neah.

No words were exchanged for several moments. Neah looked down and gave Mr. Morley a pat.

He looked up and back into Ravenna's eyes, "We have to be the best we have ever been."

Ravenna nodded in the affirmative.

## 137

Adiba continued her hacking efforts from the relative obscurity of a coffee shop in Kent, Washington. Since the encounter in Mount Carroll, direct contact was at best minimal, and always in crowded noisy places. The software that Mrs. T had provided her was extraordinary in its ability to cut through firewalls and other barricades. She had already hacked into cellphone records of Dr. Astoria along with his credit card accounts. From there his travels around the world were easy to determine.

She discovered a conundrum. Fahd was supposed to have the artifact that Rahman had collected from a private party, in fact, a relative of Bucoda. No one would suspect the fire that killed the heir was intentionally set. The other antiquities were simply thrown into the ocean near Liverpool by a deranged religious fanatic that worked for the British Royal Museum. Not only were the artifacts lost, but priceless relics from most British explorations of the Antarctic as well. Unfortunately, the materials they did have were not the most valuable objects in the universe; those were in the possession of Astoria.

## 138

Mrs. T rather enjoyed her anonymity. A witch they called her. An anomaly in the world of the Middle East. A woman of power, one who was addressed as an equal to men, but never trusted the same. Too many of her rivals disappeared. Too many of her relationships abruptly ended. While she professed her allegiance to her Arabic masters, she had another purpose, one that gathered around her like a mist, sensible by others.

She blamed the United States for all that had befallen her family, her friends, and her life. The death of her parents, her brother, and her stepmother, who was so very kind on one hand, and so very frightened of her husband on the other.

She used the face of every belief she could exploit to lash back. Mrs. T also used the military arm of the United States to her advantage. More than one of her detractors had perished by covert operations and drone strikes that she herself had called in.

Mrs. T smiled inwardly. Soon she would gain revenge, a position of world power, and wealth beyond imagining, often times promoted by the government she hated most. Any means to her goal was satisfactory, even if the Faith of Islam took the blame. Astoria was on her list, along with the pesky Neah Bey. Maybe she would kill Bey's wife first, slowly, in front of him. That would be truly satisfactory.

## 139

Kadar gathered three of his best to make his team. Two had been involved in insurgent activities in either Afghanistan or Iraq. The third was intent to the point of obsession in weapons handling. They met up in Wheat, Montana, at the co-op granary and bakery. From there they headed west on Interstate 90 in a four-wheel drive van loaded with weapons and first-aid supplies. Their intent was multi-faceted. Obtain the artifacts, bring about the end of the Western business-based world, and kill as many of the agents of the under-government as possible. An associate was bringing in a van of followers from Seattle; Portland; and Vancouver, Canada.

## 140

Fahd paced down the mall in Tukwila and paced back again. Every ten steps he looked at his watch. He frequently patted his breast pocket, continually finding assurance in the papers contained therein. While he fiddled with the small cloth bag in his pocket, it was only a tease, a bit of a puzzle, not enough to fill in all the pieces, but enough to at least garner attention.

The real prize lay with Astoria. Fahd was sure he could create the complete disaster; Kadar had made arrangements that would be the continuing effort to bring down the West. He envied Kadar and Mrs. T, both sleek, educated, professional, and focused. But it did not seem that they had lived in the rough of Tora Bora, getting shelled first by the Russians, then the factional fighting of the local warlords, and then again by the Americans. They had not seen what he had seen.

Concerning the mysterious Mrs. T, he tried to keep Kadar between himself and her. He just did not trust the woman. Odd messages he read again and again from Rahman indicated that he did not trust her either. Much later than planned, his cell phone vibrated for an incoming call. It was Mrs. T. The plan had been put into motion. Kadar had flown home to Chicago and was somewhere in Montana headed toward Seattle. *Fine*, he thought.

He swung south to Kent and picked up a woman who was introduced to him via a text message with picture. She was waiting at the curb with a small back pack. As instructed he flashed his head lights from across the intersection. The woman waved.

Fahd pulled into the bus loading turnout, and the woman slid into the passenger seat and immediately pulled a hand gun and poked it at his crotch.

"What is your real name?" she asked. To emphasize her sincerity, she cocked the hammer back on the revolver.

Fahd stared at the gun and said, "My real name is Akil Tamur. I have become Fahd."

Adiba smiled and withdrew the gun, "Good answer."

141

Budd Todd retraced the steps of things he knew. Astoria entered the United States with something that triggered the metal detectors at the Los Angeles airport. Budd obtained a court order to review the data created when

Astoria set the detector off. It was unusual, but not noteworthy enough for investigation. The signature could be traced. Video taken from the security cameras showed a hearse being loaded with a coffin at the airport. He called some friends over at NEST. They decided to cooperate outside of regular office hours at Todd's house.

Randle and Perry showed up, one with a case of Corona, the other with three Papa Murphy's pizzas. The colonel wheeled in from the patio and cranked up the oven. Perry sat at the table after going back to the Tahoe-SUV and began setting up a laptop and projector. Todd thumbtacked a sheet to the wall and closed the blinds. Randle cracked eight beers and sliced the limes, stabbing a chunk into the necks of each of the Coronas. In a few minutes the oven was at temperature, and the colonel shoved two of the pizzas in.

"Well, you gimpy goat humper, what is on your pathetically small brain today?" Randle smiled at Budd Todd.

Perry chugged down one beer and reached for another. "That is a terrible thing to say to a superior officer, you fudge-packing leper."

Todd sat down at the table with a beer in each hand. "Oh, didn't I mention we are not to talk shop here, you urinal-licking perverts."

The colonel smiled broadly from his custom wheelchair, "Dear God I miss the camaraderie of active duty. Which is something none of you pansy inbreds had to deal with."

Todd rolled his eyes over at the colonel, "Jeez, Gramps, tell us about the Spanish-American war, again, and again, and again."

The screen flickered on. Smiles were replaced by frowns, the bubbles in the untouched beers slowly rose to the bottle necks. Todd took a laser pointer and placed the spot on LAX. "Here is the trace starting point." He plugged in a USB drive and brought up the signature taken from the airport. "This is the target; show me your magic."

Perry and Randle began linking up with the NEST mainframe. The firewall failed miserably and they were in. Data streamed across the sheet. Suddenly a dot appeared just north of L.A., and then another further north, and another. "Eureka! We got it." Randle shouted.

The colonel studied the screen, "Okay, you tracked it, how? Where are the detectors?"

Perry smiled and said, "Have you ever noticed funny boxes by the freeway?"

The colonel frowned, "Dude, I see all kinds of funny stuff by the freeway. What kind of funny boxes are you talking about?"

Randle hit a few keys, "How about these funny boxes?" Several images of black and dark brown rectangular boxes, about two feet by two feet with the flat side pointed toward the traffic appeared.

"Yeah, I've seen those boxes. What are they?" The colonel asked.

Perry chimed in, "Those, my friends, are the NEST boxes. You will find them all along the freeways, north-south, and east-west. They are everywhere. About twenty-five hundred right now, more every month." He brought up a map showing the United States road system. Dots appeared along the roads, rings of dots around Washington, D.C., New York, L.A., and more. "You will observe that at every major interchange you will see dots. At high-value targets you will see more." He circled the obvious locations of the Pentagon, Fort Knox, and Quantico. Also circled was the Hanford Reservation, once part of the Manhattan Project. Todd squinted at the ring of dots surrounding the Hanford Reservation, an area he was familiar with.

Todd asked, "You are worried about radioactive materials being taken into." His voice trailed off, "Oh, or out of, I suppose."

Randle smiled, "Yeah, we are concerned about threats coming in, as well as materials being taken out."

Perry had entered the search parameters into his laptop and changed the projector cable over. "Here we are, kiddies, the track of your mystery object." It followed the route of the hearse north to Washington State. Detector stations grew thin in Eastern Washington. One dot appeared north of Spokane, near the small town of Metaline Falls.

Todd stared at the screen. "Can you layer the data by time?"

Randle keyed in the parameters. Dots took on a rainbow of colors. "The last black dot is the one you see at, what's that place? Metallica Falls?"

The colonel laughed, "You Air Force rejects live in a gilded cage, that's Metaline Falls."

Todd ignored the exchange and commented, "It went there, and it didn't come back. Where is the next detector north of there?" Randle added layers to the map. Since Metaline Falls lay on a small highway north of Spokane, there were several detectors closer to the Canadian border.

"Zip. Package did not go north, or south, so logic says the package is in Metaline Falls."

The colonel sipped on his beer, "What is your accuracy percentage of this data?"

Randle said, "It's 99.9 percent accurate. We have to be

as close to perfect as we can be. Simply put, we cannot have radioactive materials in transit around the country. So far we have been perfect in intercepts."

The colonel asked, "Does that mean radioactive material has been brought in before? How come we weren't told?" He alternated his frown from Perry to Randle and back again.

Randle and Perry turned both their computers off. "We can neither confirm nor deny the existence of such instances occurring." Perry handed the colonel a pocket pen dosimeter. The colonel pointed it at the overhead light. "Oh. Who took that hit?" The dosimeter showed a very high, most likely, fatal reading. Whoever wore the dosimeter was already dead or nearly so.

Perry frowned and lowered his head, "That was mine."

Wheeler pushed his chair closer to where Perry sat, he placed a hand on the younger man's shoulder, "I'm sure sorry, son."

142

Kadar studied the map. Mrs. T had impressive resources, the NEST data scrolled over the laptop screen. "Okay, at Spokane, we head north."

143

Fahd was headed east and got the text message; he plugged in the name Metaline Falls into his GPS and stepped down on the accelerator.

He had a meeting with a man named Haytham at a car lot in Spokane where he would get rid of Adiba. He was never sure that she had un-cocked the revolver.

## 144

Mrs. T tapped the pilot on the shoulder and made a circular motion with her finger. The helicopter blades began to rotate.

## 145

Dr. Dayton Astoria excused himself from the table and walked out on to the patio. He saw the basalt obelisks and the rough bench. It only took a moment to walk there. He was able to use his phone and send a text message without being detected.

## 146

Ravenna Lakota got a very strange message. It was simple. "We are coming to the party, like it or not."

## 147

Ione held Neah's hand. "I'm going with you this time. If nothing else, I'll look after Dr. Astoria. He seems a little needy."

## 148

The text message from Dr. Astoria was received. The four-wheel drive Jeep Wrangler began the corkscrew descent from the Lion's Lookout south of Wenatchee.

## 149

Neah drove through the light snow falling most of the way from Snoqualmie Pass to the Highway 231 cutoff. Ravenna sat in the rear seat chatting intermittently with Dr. Astoria, who seemed to be pensive. Behind them, in the cargo area of the SUV, was a collection of electronic equipment and weapons.

Neah checked the GPS frequently. Ione sensed that tension was building and could not think of anything to do to help.

## 150

The colonel wheeled in and parked next to Budd. Budd looked up, and saw a strange look in the colonel's face. It raised memories from long ago, in fact, the day he lost his legs.

"Colonel?" The colonel leaned forward, "Think you can still handle a gun?" Todd asked. Over the colonel's shoulder appeared Perry and Randle. Budd Todd, smiling from ear to ear, lowered his head and began screwing his legs on.

The colonel scowled at the team, "I know you pansies think that I am so old that the last gun I used was a flintlock, but it just ain't so. Stick around, you might just learn something."

### 151

Madison's mother laid a bundle of flowers on her son's grave. A light skiff of snow lay in the grass hummocks between the plots. Spring was a little late this year, not uncommon for the Ponderosa forest of Northeast Washington.

### 152

The Jeep Wrangler pulled backwards up a retired logging road that overlooked the cemetery. It reversed back up the hill until it was hidden from view.

### 153

Neah looked over his shoulder at Dr. Astoria, "Well, Doctor, we are here. Tell us what we need to do."

Astoria looked out over the small town. "Seems so peaceful. Like some kind of Currier and Ives painting on a cookie tin."

Ravenna nodded. "Let's hope it stays that way."

Ione reached over the seat and patted Astoria's arm. "We'll be fine, right Neah?" Neah's facial expression did not inspire confidence. The SUV pulled into the cemetery entrance. There was a single car in the parking lot.

"Oh, crap, I know that car!" Astoria slipped down in the seat. "That's Madison's mother's car! We can't stay here!" Neah calmly put the SUV in reverse and backed out of the parking lot.

"Good catch, Doc. It's early, we have time." Neah was backing up the access road.

They drove up to the Canadian border and returned about noon. The clouds had parted, letting in the sunlight. It was still cold enough to see their breaths as they solemnly walked toward the grave. Astoria slowed his walk, as if somehow being repelled by an invisible force from the grave. Ravenna cast a look around the area and then set down a Pelican case. She laid it over on its side and pulled back a Velcro cover. An external switch was activated and the ground-penetrating radar began electronically cutting through the earth over Madison's grave. Ravenna slowly pushed the case just inside the still-visible grass cut left there from when the grave was dug.

The monitor clarified the image in a remarkable manner. Beneath their feet the radar returned a signal that identified the edge of the casket. Metal fittings could be seen, they were the hinges, the locking mechanisms, and sadly there was the outline of Madison's corpse.

Astoria wiped tears from his eyes. "Sorry, my friend, I'm really sorry."

Ione put her hand on Astoria's shoulder. "Don't worry, they will be careful, and it will be over soon." Ravenna stopped pushing the case. A sharply defined image came back of four metallic parts. The image was vastly different from the casket fittings. Ravenna nodded at Neah.

Neah craned his neck around and looked. "Okay, this part gets a little, well, difficult. So why don't Dayton and Ione follow me back to the rig while I gather the gear?"

Astoria's face flushed an angry red. "What do you think you are going to do?" He stepped forward chin out thrust and hands clenched into fists. Ravenna knew that Bey was not one to be fainthearted this close to a goal. She stepped between the two men. Out of the corner of her eye she saw Neah slide his right hand back. He was setting up to draw his .45.

She thought to herself that while Neah had numerous talents and abilities to bring to any harrowing situation, patience was not his long suit.

"Doctor, please, I promise we will be respectful. It is our intent to leave no evidence of our visit. Please?" She placed a hand on Astoria's shoulder and gently pushed.

Ione whispered, "Neah? You will be careful? You promise?"

Neah, out-flanked, stepped back and folded his hands in front of him. "I promise." Astoria gave one last look at Madison's headstone and walked away; Ione had hooked his arm.

Bey took a step forward to collect the gear from the SUV, but Ravenna turned and cut him off. "Jackass," was all she said and then pushed him back with a strong arm. "I'll get the tools." Neah, with nothing better to do, scanned the tree line.

## 154

They were well hidden, tucked behind logs and rocks, waiting. After scouting Madison's grave, they took up positions when Mrs. T informed them that an SUV was headed their way. She had parked the chopper on the back side of a ridge line overlooking the town. The evening prior she had set up a remote battery-operated camera that used a cell phone signal to relay to her images of the highway on the south side of Metaline Falls.

Fahd hefted the AK, as he had done for years; it was like shaking hands with an old friend. He nodded to Kadar, indicating that he should hang back with his associates, becoming an effective blocker to cut off the highway or the road to the cemetery. Fahd would have preferred his traditional clothing over the American jacket and jeans; there were just not enough places to carry extra magazines for the AK.

## 155

Ravenna brought out the drill; it was disassembled in a duffle bag. The drill and bit were a little heavy to haul around, really more cumbersome than heavy. Neah and Ravenna began putting the motor on the shaft. From time to time the clouds would darken the skies.

Ravenna's cell phone vibrated. She looked at Neah and then at the phone. Nether agent spoke; they left the drill on the ground partially assembled and began slowly walking back to the SUV. Neah, while holding his head fixed on the SUV, scanned his eyes to the right as far as he could without turning his head. Ravenna was replicating his stance but looked as far as she could to the left. When they got within ten feet of the SUV, one of Kadar's associates stood up and shot wildly at them. The bullets whistled overhead and cracked into the straight trunks of the towering Ponderosa pines. Neah pulled his .45 and fired rapidly in the direction of the muzzle blasts.

Ravenna made it to the SUV and dove into the driver's seat. In a second the big V8 roared to life. By this time Neah was in the passenger seat shouting at Ione and Astoria to get down. Bullets plowed into the heavy rig as the hidden dangerous confederates rose and opened fire. Fahd and Kadar ran toward the drill. Ravenna backed the SUV up the small hill onto the highway and smoked the tires heading south. About a half mile down the road, Ravenna slammed on the brakes. Neah bailed out. From a special compartment built into the door of the SUV he withdrew an M-16 with a collapsible stock and shortened barrel, and then without saying anything darted into the woods.

Ravenna turned to Ione and Astoria, "Stay with the truck!" She ran farther down the road, past Bey's entry point into the forest and disappeared into the forest about two hundred yards before the cemetery access road.

Astoria looked at Ione, "Is-Is-Is?" he stuttered.

Ione looked at the stricken doctor, "Is this normal? I don't think so." Overhead a helicopter could be heard chewing through the cold air.

## 156

Fahd and Kadar grabbed the drill and sized up the ground radar image. The drill was electric, very quiet and very powerful. It ground down through the partially frozen soil, only bogging down when it hit the casket screws and bolts. In two minutes Fahd was on his belly with the remote camera that was part of the ground radar unit. It had a small snare that grabbed the bag in which he would find the power to ascend to greatness few could dream of.

He pulled the bag from the hole and smiled at Kadar. "We have it! We have it!" A black helicopter landed a few yards from the grave site, sending ice chunks outward, pummeling the two men.

## 157

Ravenna arrived at the tree line bordering on the cemetery and fell behind a log as the bullets from one of Kadar's associates ripped into the trees and duff after having spotted her running through the forest. She hunkered down as best she could as dozens of rounds chipped away at the log.

Neah raised the M-16 and fired at the smoke puffs coming out of the underbrush. The shooter turned his attention to the new threat, allowing Ravenna to raise the MP-5. A short burst and the shooting stopped. There was no reprieve when others of Kadar's team began honing in on Ravenna and Bey's positions with weapons fire.

## 158

The helicopter door flew open, and Mrs. T and a man jumped out, crouching low to avoid the rotors and presenting less of a target. She waved Fahd and Kadar toward the helicopter.

They met behind some headstones. "Do you have it?" she shouted.

Fahd raised the bag and shouted, "We have it! There are more parts than we had hoped for!"

She waved both Kadar and Fahd to the chopper. "Get out of here now! We will take care of everything else." The man accompanying Mrs. T used a headstone to steady a sniper rifle and fired a shot at Neah Bey.

## 159

Bey twisted from pain as the slug nipped his shoulder. "God damn, that just healed up!" He spied Ravenna edging further away from him, trying to establish a cross fire. More bullets tore up the trees and forest floor around him. They were getting flanked from the cemetery and the high ground that held the road to the cemetery. The helicopter roared off to the west.

## 160

Budd Todd relayed the battle facts to the colonel. "Got it, bro. I'm dialing now." It was rumored Wheeler had contacts everywhere, and Budd was glad he was calling for support.

Budd shifted the heavy Garand and fired across the open cemetery. He let the stricken man scream for a while before taking the head shot.

## 161

A special phone rang at the Portland Air National Guard Wing on the flight line. The Duty Officer set his coffee down and marked the time on his log sheet. "This had better be good." was the greeting from the Redhawks Fighter Group headquartered there. The officer took notes and motioned to the two duty pilots. In his excitement he stood and waved in earnest at the pilots, indicating with hand gestures that they needed to run to their planes. He made a trigger finger and pulled it repeatedly and pointed toward the flight line.

The two pilots ran toward their planes, held ready 24 hours a day. They were airborne in less than seven minutes.

"Redhawks, this is Vampire, orders?"

"Redhawks, this is Firebreather, orders?" The two pilots checked in.

"Vampire, Firebreather, this is a danger close, known hostiles, Northeast Washington, weapons hot, your discretion. Expedite delivery." Both pilots looked at each other, separated by mere feet. They advanced the throttles to full military power. The pilots were thrown back into the cockpit seats. Dancing diamonds erupted from the engines. By the time they hit their crossing just up river from Camas, they were supersonic.

Emergency call centers recorded in excess of one hundred and fifty thousand calls from the eastern metropolitan area of Portland, Oregon, to Vancouver, Washington, in less than two minutes as the sonic booms rattled windows, dishes, and nerves.

162

With the call for air support completed, the colonel spoke to Budd, "Okay peg-legs, let's go be heroes."

Budd looked back at his friend and said, "Again."

The colonel looked down from his perch and nudged Budd. "Time to dish out some pain, I think."

Budd placed an M-16 in the colonel's hands. He draped his shoulder with an old .30-06 Garand fitted with a large scope. "Yeah, let's open that old can of whoop-ass." As the colonel pointed off to his right and slowly rolled down the asphalt, Budd began picking his way through the pines in the direction indicated by the colonel.

Both men hunched their shoulders forward, lowered their chins, and in spite of their handicaps, waged a fight they were trained to do. Incoming rounds threw up bark chunks, shattered rock, and passed overhead; these they ignored. Every muzzle blast directed into their position was answered round for round. They gave up nothing.

163

As the helicopter blasted over the trees, Fahd could see Bey crouching behind a tree. He stuck the AK out of the window and used the frame as a brace. He emptied the magazine.

### 164

Neah was hit in the thigh by a round and then pummeled by exploding granite and basalt rocks blown apart by the slugs; splinters of pine blown off stuck in his shoulder and back. He rolled over and shot wildly at the shape of the chopper flying overhead. He missed. A sniper having watched the exploding terrain used this data to make Neah's position. The cross hairs lined up on Neah's torso, he squeezed off the round.

### 165

Mrs. T ran off to Neah's left, making the tree line two-hundred meters distant in near Olympic time.

### 166

Ravenna kept on pushing to her right; she needed to line up a shot on the sniper pounding at Neah. With a gasp of pain, she fell to the ground. Her calf was pierced, fountaining blood from the ruptured tissue. More shots landed close by, slapping into the adjacent trees and tearing up the forest floor.

## 167

Neah rolled down the hill to a spot of relative safety behind a huge stone pushed from the cemetery decades before. He grabbed a pain pill and chomped down on it. "God Damn!" was all he could say.

As the M-16 was being raised into firing position so Neah could get a shot at the man shooting at Ravenna, the center of the M-16 disassembled into broken flying plastic and metal fragments. The sniper's round destroyed the long gun in a blinding flash of sparks and molten metal. Neah's face and neck were ripped with hot shards.

## 168

Ravenna tore her pant leg down and tied a compression dressing over the hole.

## 169

The pilots were formed into a two-plane echelon, with Vampire in the lead plane. Their engines shredded the air, and a following wave of sonic booms traced their path north of Vancouver, banking east between Mount Adams and Mount St. Helens. From there it was a scant few minutes where they re-crossed the Columbia River near Vantage.

"Redhawks, Vampire and Firebreather, you copy?" It was a voice unfamiliar to both the pilots.

"Copy, who are you?"

The colonel spoke directly. "I am your forward air controller; Wheeler is the handle. Prepare for mission."

Vampire looked over at Firebreather; she shrugged her shoulders and gave thumbs up. Firebreather repeated the gesture. "We copy, go."

The colonel watched the helicopter disappear to the west. "Pilots, chopper, black, west heading, angels 2, northwest your flight."

Both pilots looked at their displays. "Copy, Wheeler, mission?"

The colonel keyed the mic, "Very unfriendlies in rotary, possessing material detrimental to interests of the United States. Eliminate with prejudice." He paused keeping the mic button depressed. Soft static filled the pilot's ears. "Make it hurt, and make it last."

### 170

Vampire smiled. An injury at the Air Force Academy required dental surgery to correct. She thought having very small silver tips on her upper canines was hot. Vampire took her mask off and smiled over to Firebreather. He grimaced; nothing peaceful ensued when she made that terrifying smile. He made a gesture pointing toward heaven. She put her mask back on. They pushed the throttles again hoping to close the distance faster. They tipped their noses upward and screamed into the sky. Afterburners ignited, and twin columns of blue flame erupted from the massive engines.

## 171

Sprague Palmer shut the tractor down on the flat lands north of Metaline. The big diesel rumbled to a stop, finally letting the light breeze become the only sound he heard. He stepped from the cab of the big John Deere; the 8295R began to buffet a little from the wind coming up the valley. He climbed down to the ground, taking a quick walk around the machine, checking for debris and looking to see if he had picked up any old fence material that might snag something. Sprague pushed and pulled the hitch assembly, making sure it was still fast. A little late spring tilling was needed to prep some of his three-thousand-acre farm for planting. Some of the lands were rolling hills, some in pasture, and some in Ponderosa forest.

He looked up and to the southwest; two high fast-moving black dots caught his eye. As a former member of a forward air control unit, he knew what they were. As a Delta Force SCUD hunter, he also knew what to expect. Sprague Palmer faced the oncoming fighter jets, spread his arms, and closed his eyes. He let the sonic boom wash over him.

In seconds his wife Merritt called, fretting; she did not know what the noise was from. Memories from his Delta Force past began to seep in around him, like spectral whispers he did not want to hear.

Merritt was then worried that the noise might create a flashback, a random PTSD episode. She hedged around, not wishing to pry, but not wishing to be uncaring. Sprague knew what his wife was asking. His eyes tried to find the final dots of light indicating vast amounts of hydrocarbons were being consumed at an astonishing rate.

"No, honey, I'm fine. Someone is just going somewhere very fast. Very odd that they broke the sound barrier over land here. Why don't you look up where the President is?" He gazed to the northeast, trying to get one last glimpse of the fighters.

In a moment she called back, "Sprague, the President is in Florida, what does that have to do with the sonic boom?"

He laughed softly, "Well, usually something must be going on for the fighters to get called out, and then something must be going wrong in a big way for them to break the sound barrier, especially over the continental United States. I think it's even against the law."

There was a pause. In the distance to the northeast, he could make out the tracers arcing across the sky. "Uh, Merritt, why don't you meet me at the old home site with the rig? I think we should visit your brother at the mine."

"I am leaving now." She hung up the phone and quickly text-messaged her brother. When Sprague wanted to be in the lower galleries of an old gold mine on the property where her brother lived, it meant he was feeling vulnerable. The massive stone provided a measure of security and "lack of distant horizons" his V.A. doctor said was important for him to find his center.

In reality, he just liked having a few hundred million pounds of rock and dirt over his head. This meant that he did not have to fear someone laying a set of cross hairs on his chest from 500 yards out.

## 172

Perry studied the report for the last time. It was a death sentence described in the strange prose of the language of the medical world. His radiation exposure had killed him, of that five different doctors from five different clinics or hospitals had spoken.

It had been a simple call, a suspicious package, a strange reading, and then all hell broke loose. The package was a ruse; the real radioactive source was behind them. Perry took his time and photographed, sketched, measured, and then finally decided that they could move the mystery package to the disposal truck. By then the radioactive source had done its damage.

A disgruntled employee had stolen the radioactive source used in industrial radiography of heavy-walled piping. The employee had rigged up an electronic shutter on a cell phone switch. When he saw the NEST group examine the phony device, he trigged the real device. Not that it was much satisfaction; the FBI entry team shot him dead three days later when he charged them from his apartment.

Perry stabbed himself in the arm with enough Phenobarbitals to stun an elk. He barely felt it. With practiced skill he donned his camouflage face paint.

## 173

The van ground to a halt in the cemetery parking lot, and six of Kadar's followers dispersed. They were given orders to cover the escape of Kadar, and then flee and meet in Seattle. Kadar considered them expendable in this grand cause; he did not expect them to survive.

## 174

Neah gasped in pain; it took an effort to get his feet under him. He pulled a blood-stained shard of pine from his upper back. Of the several, it was the only one he could reach. The pill washed over him. He picked his way toward the southern border of the cemetery.

A crackle of automatic weapons sounded to his right. Ravenna was evening the odds. He rested against a tree and watched the van empty its contents. "Crap" was all he could muster as the men dashed into the trees to the north and south of the parking lot. "Well, guess I'll earn my pay today." He looked up the hill towards the SUV, but could not see the vehicle or his wife.

The smashed M-16 lay at his feet. All he had left was his .45 hand weapon.

With his right shoulder blade pinned against his ribs by the splinter of pine, he was forced to use his left hand, his off hand, to handle the big automatic. One of Kadar's men jumped up and fired wildly. It took half a magazine from the .45 to bring the man down.

## 175

Ravenna got the temporary bandage wrapped around her leg and edged forward, eyes scanning the terrain. A round passed by her head, missing her, but revealing the position of the shooter. She lined up the sights from the thin cover of some forest brush. She waited to refine her shot.

It did not take long. If the shooter had remained still he might have gone unnoticed, but he moved the barrel using the scope to find her. It was a fatal mistake. A three-round burst killed him. She crawled over to his position and examined the rifle to see if it would help her.

## 176

Vampire pointed at Firebreather to descend. He rolled over and dove earthward. Their radars lit up the helicopter from over a hundred miles out. They closed the distance in seconds.

## 177

Kadar pointed from the copilot's seat toward the two jets as they split, one rocketing up, and other rolling under them. The lower plane leveled off and passed just under the helicopter. The jet wash rocked them.

Fahd screamed, "Down, down, we have to land!"

Kadar watched the twin horizontal tongues of fire recede to the east. He turned to the pilot and laughed, "They missed us!" The pilot jerked the chopper up as Vampire swept under them from the opposite direction.

"No! No! We have to go down!" Fahd screamed over the roar of the helicopter engine. But then Firebreather had swung around and forced the chopper higher yet.

The pilot tried to roll to the south, but the sky in front of the chopper filled with tracer fire. He rolled away only to find that Vampire was under him again, and again he had to gain altitude to avoid the wash that would surely knock them from the sky.

The dance continued until the helicopter rotors could not get enough bite in the thin air. The pilot frantically looked around him for any means of escape. Kadar and Fahd searched in all directions for the jets. It was very difficult to breathe; the men strained taking in large gulps of air. It was forced into their lungs with great effort, and they gulped and held their lungs under tension in hopes it would drive the waning amounts of oxygen into their systems.

Vampire and Firebreather were not affected by the lack of oxygen in the least, they were however thrown about the cockpits of the jets and repeatedly crushed under massive G forces. Each hard turn, each slamming of the throttles forward, each ignition of the afterburners stressed their hearts, lungs, eyes, and brains. Shoulder joints were stretched, necks torqued, lower backs pummeled, and with each pass they tightened the noose.

178

Perry stalked his prey with ruthless precision. The Olympic competition compound bow was heavy, but he loved it nevertheless. Silently moving through the forest, he gave away nothing. The Phenobarbital began to fail to stave off the pain; he knew time was running out, the first step in what the doctors told him would be his final moments. Standing with his eyes closed for a moment allowed him to focus, to bring himself back to the mission, to the here and the now. He looked at the syringes filled with painkillers and muscle relaxers and decided to face his foreshortened future without them.

## 179

The homegrown terrorist from Minneapolis fired a dozen rounds at Neah Bey. He was sure he had hit him. It was an amateur's mistake to give up his position so soon after firing. Using a short tree limb, he steadied the rifle to get in another shot at Bey. He brought the cross hairs up and centered them on Bey's side as he lay near a large stone. There was an intense pain, a crushing sensation on his chest. It was as if a bolt of lightning passed through his torso, and then darkness from all edges of his vision.

## 180

Perry released the arrow forty yards out. It was an easy kill. The arrow entered under the right armpit of his quarry and exited under his left. The arrow sank deeply into the tree, pinning the dead man there. Perry walked by, not even giving the dead man a second glance. He knocked another of his custom arrows, the ones he used on black ops drug interdiction missions in Central America. He ghosted from tree and bush and stone to stand nearly in front of his next prey who was foolishly focused elsewhere.

## 181

Mrs. T watched Ravenna slink off to engage the van's occupants. Her desire was to take on the infamous Neah Bey. She edged around the cemetery's southern edge. Mrs. T felt she was better than Bey and was eager to close the distance between them. Reaching behind her, she patted the special leather sleeve that held her favorite knife in line with her spine.

## 182

They stopped the SUV and jumped out. Ione grabbed a pair of binoculars and was horror struck to see Neah fall down under a hail of bullets. She was only slightly relieved to see him roll to the shelter of a rock. "We have to help them!" she shouted at Astoria.

Astoria shrugged his shoulders, "Uh, this really isn't in my resume, but tell me what to do!" They stood at the back of the SUV and raised the rear hatch. A variety of firearms and ammunition were laid out in order. They stared at the collection trying to decide what to do.

Massive hands landed on each of their shoulders from behind.

## 183

Merritt breathed out a sigh of relief as she saw her husband leaning against a fence post down at the old farm access road. *So far, so good*, she thought. He was up and smiling at her as he walked toward the pickup truck. She pointed at the steering wheel and frowned. He shook his head "No" and got in the passenger seat. "Hiya, sweetie! I'm good with you driving for a bit." He closed the door, and asked, "Did you get in touch with Blanca or Padden at the mine?"

Merritt engaged the transmission of the big Ford FX4 and set off down the farm road, "Yes, they said you are always welcome to explore the old mine." She smiled at Sprague. He nodded his head and fiddled with the radio to see if he could find some 1960's rock and roll from Pandora off his cell phone. They both knew why he was headed to the mine. They played this "distancing game" which was part of the healing process, the doctor at the VA told them.

"For the time being, whatever you want to call the trips to the mine is okay. We will need to cross that bridge of being open and accepting of the real reason someday." The doctor was always supportive, and, in spite of the reputation of the VA, always answered the phone, even in the middle of the night, on weekends, or holidays.

They drove east, finally hitting the highway and began heading north for a few miles' ride to the turnoff for her brother and sister-in-law's farm. The mine was only a few hundred feet deep but at such an angle that it burrowed its way deep into the solid rock. Few, if any, timbers were needed to support the narrow tunnel and its collection of small galleries.

Blanca and Padden had been with Merritt when Sprague came home. They visited him at the hospital and even took him there many times over the years when Merritt was uncertain of driving the icy roads of Northeastern Washington. They were glad that Sprague was doing better. He was a great guy when he was "on his game" as he said, and very quiet and reclusive when "not home."

Over the years Sprague had confided in Padden what he had been exposed to in the SCUD hunts. He told Padden that he "was on the ass end of the universe for days on end, limited water, little food, and constantly under threat." He did two tours and was in the process of signing up for a third when he "broke."

He never revealed what it was that "broke" him, but it had to do with coming up on armed children. Several armed children. Several armed children being ordered into combat by a fanatical man. In the ensuing melee, the only survivors were Sprague, his team, and the fanatic that left the children to die while he ran away. A brief note was made in a report; scant mention was made of the fifteen shallow graves left behind.

Sprague suffered; the doctor said to Merritt during one bad spell that he "lacked closure." Sprague would heal or never heal; it was up to him.

184

Vampire rolled out of the last run and made a cross-hands "X" in front of her in the cockpit. Firebreather clicked his mic twice in acknowledgement. He stood the war bird on its tail and slammed the throttles forward. Vampire rolled away and dropped her landing gear and speed brake to reduce her speed. She waited circling under the chopper, like a sky shark, waiting to strike. Firebreather punched through twenty-five thousand feet and looped backwards, never taking his eyes off the chopper.

## 185

The chopper pilot looked up, and then tipped the machine over on its side and looked down. He steadied the machine level and lowered his chin to his chest and began praying.

## 186

Firebreather lowered his landing gear and deployed his speed brake. In the ears of the pilots a distant voice said, "Well done, Vampire and Firebreather, make them burn." Slowly the one jet fell, slowly the other jet rose from beneath. When the jets were equidistant from the rotors, they fired short bursts from their guns. The outer two-thirds of the rotors flew off in wild disarray. Vampire and Firebreather retracted their landing gear and air brakes. In seconds they were wing tip to wing tip above the stricken helicopter.

## 187

With the rotor blades gone, the helicopter engine over-sped. The transmission was never designed to sustain such excessive forces, and it failed. Molten metal shot from the engine compartment and severed hydraulic fluid and fuel lines. The entire passenger compartment filled with dense smoke and thick orange flames. Fahd screamed and forced open the door and exited from the burning helicopter. Kadar shouted to the pilot, "Do something!!" He turned to see why his command went unanswered; the pilot had an engine part embedded in the back of his head. Kadar fought the door next to the copilot's seat until the Plexiglas melted and flowed over and encased his arms. Held in nearly molten plastic, he was prevented from moving at all. On the floor board next to him sat the bag of prized parts. The fire burned the bag away, and shortly the parts melted into useless puddles. There was little he could do except look out the open hole and stare at Fahd floating just an arm's length away, on fire.

The two bodies, the helicopter, and Fahd, having different drag rates, separated by a few yards. Kadar watched as Lake Roosevelt grew larger and larger. Fahd landed just shy of the shore line, impacting the snow-covered columnar basalt that lined that part of the lake.

188

---

Perry let fly the arrow; it pierced the man right through the heart from the front and exited out through the rib cage in the back. Stunned, the victim looked down at the blood pouring from his chest. In amazement he looked around, but all he saw was the Cheshire-Cat grin of Perry standing less than ten feet away. He sagged to his knees and died. Perry turned slowly and walked on to the where other shots were coming from.

## 189

The colonel rolled on the pneumatic tires into the parking lot. Gravity was his friend; he could keep the rifle in motion. An adversary startled from the bushes to his left, and perished with a double body tap.

Budd rested the old Garand on a bean bag he brought with him. It made anything an excellent rest for the big gun. From where he lay he took out three of the van's tires. An attacker rose and fired at Budd. A single round to the head dropped him.

## 190

Ione gasped, and Astoria spun around, the heavy hands withdrew. "Hi, Doc! Howya doing?" A hand extended toward Ione Bey. "My name's Everett Pierce, who are you?"

Astoria stood flabbergasted, "Ev-Ev-Ev..." Everett shook Ione's hand,

"Well, the Doc here was never known to be much on speeches, huh?" The big man said.

Ione weakly smiled, "So you know each other?" Her hand disappeared in the grasp of Pierce's massive paw. She feared her hand would be crushed, but the large man seemed cognizant of his size and strength.

Astoria nodded to the affirmative, "Yes, Everett is my right hand on all the expeditions."

Everett looked into the trunk. "My, Doctor, you have been hanging around with an interesting lot, I see." A smattering of shots echoed from below them. Everett glanced down the hill and back to the pair. "The lady all dressed in black and the old guy are the good guys here?" Ione and Astoria nodded.

"Well, why don't you two stay right here and watch the road, and let me lend a hand." Mostly hidden by the massive frame of Everett Pierce was the Barrett .50 caliber rifle. He pulled a camouflaged neckerchief over his face and in spite of his size, quietly drifted down the hill.

"Of course, Ma'am, if you know how to use that M-16, some cover fire would be appreciated from time to time?" Pierce spoke over his shoulder.

Ione grabbed the assault rifle and slammed a thirty-round magazine home and released the bolt. "Can do."

Astoria grabbed a sling containing extra magazines, "I guess these are important?"

Ione nodded.

191

They watched the burning human impact the ground and the flaming helicopter plow into Lake Roosevelt. It was hundreds of feet deep there.

They each performed a slow victory roll over the cemetery. They went wing tip to wing tip for a moment, then Firebreather rolled away and came back upside down, their canopies only feet apart. They sped westward, returning to base. Vampire looked up at Firebreather and gave him a 'thumbs up' sign. Firebreather repeated the gesture and rolled away. They again formed the two plane echelon and flew on into the gathering sunset.

## 192

Perry knew what was happening; they had warned him. The cancer would eventually eat into a major blood supply, and he would bleed out internally. He felt the vessel wall give away, and his strength began to fade. Still, this last adversary was more aware of his environment than the others. Perry slowly sidestepped across the open space between them. He had heard the click-click of the rifle being loaded. A dark cloud crossed the sun for a moment. Perry had waited patiently, though his strength was ebbing.

Three silent steps and he was above the man who was now using a monocular to scan the cemetery below. Perry's arm twitched, his grip fading as each pound of his heart bled him further out. His gut seemed to be filling up. Perry took a last breath and pulled the bow string taut. The arrow struck home just under the occiput of the victim.

Perry sat down under a tall Ponderosa pine, clutched a pendant that held a picture of his parents, and died.

## 193

The soft sounds of footfalls came upon the scene. Randall looked down and said, "Good bye, my friend." He used his draw hand to close the vacant eyes. His Ghilly suit blended perfectly with the forest. His bow was shrouded with an intricate netting of pine needles and bark. Already he had expended a few arrows of his own. Tears traced through his camo makeup.

## 194

Ravenna choked down a pain pill and crept slowly forward. Her anger about getting shot fed a fire burning inside her. The foolish man thought that since Ravenna was a woman he could take her on hand to hand. He did knock the gun from her hand. That only angered Ravenna Lakota even more. From a distance it sounded like someone beating a sack of potatoes with a baseball bat. Except for the screaming.

## 195

Mrs. T and Neah met in a small clearing. Neah sagged to his knees, his vision blurring from sweat, pain, and blood loss. His right shoulder fixed into place by a splinter of pine.

"Well, you must be the famous Neah Bey. I expected more, you know." She smiled.

Neah wiped the blood from his face with his left forearm. "Yeah, me, too."

She continued smiling at him, "Ah, witty to the end." She raised the gun, centering the muzzle at his heart.

Neah grinned slowly; blood stained his teeth and colored his lips, "Do you know what the difference is between me and you?"

Mrs. T grinned, "Why, yes I do. I'm going to live, and you are going to die." She was oblivious to a red dot which began tracing its way to her midsection.

Neah frowned, "No, not really." He sagged to his left hand. Straining his neck, he looked up.

Mrs. T asked, "Then, Mr. Neah Bey, what is the difference between me and you?" She cocked the gun.

Neah stared into the eyes of Mrs. T and said, "Friends."

"Friends? Really Mr. Bey, I had expected something more profound in your final moments!" She slid the pistol into the holster at her side and from her mid back drew out a stout blade with a stag horn handle. "Well, Neah, since we are friends, but just for a moment more, I will use my old friend here to send you to hell." The red dot held steady on her breast bone. Mrs. T flew into a multitude of parts and pieces. The 500 grain, all-lead slug from the Barrett shattered her instantly. Bey's hair was tousled as the round passed less than an inch over his head. He fell face first into unconsciousness.

## 196

Seven hundred yards away Everett Pierce folded up the bipod on the Barrett. "One shot, one kill." He smiled at no one. "I still got the magic." He loaded another massive shell into the Barrett and searched for another target. The stealth of the huge man was remarkable as he stepped through the brush.

A crack of a rifle shot froze him into a block of muscle and bone. He tilted his head from side to side, ranging with his eyes for motion and his ears for sound. Little escaped his study of the terrain.

The motion of a hand trying to part the underbrush revealed a target, a target ranging him in equal steadfastness. The huge Barrett rose up, connected to the man. They were one. A roar and flash erupted; a trail of light snow was disturbed along the flight path of the round. Again a mist of red flowered hundreds of yards away.

From over his head a dozen rounds from Ione's assault rifle splintered brush across the open cemetery, identifying a target for Pierce.

He stepped forward, again, the feral man hunting other feral men.

A shadow from the low sun indicated through the high-powered scope that someone was setting up a shot at a man in a wheelchair a half mile away. A twelve-inch ponderosa pine shielding the man from direct view toppled when the massive round bored through it. The victim was pierced multiple times by the wood splinters through the midsection along with the remnants of the huge slug.

### 197

And so the battle raged, the wisps of arrows through the foliage terminating in the crack of bone and the tearing of flesh, the sharp crackle of small arms fire, the roar of the big gun, and the utter destruction of others.

### 198

Astoria shouted, "Down the road!"

A camouflaged figure darted down the shoulder of the road, intent on circling Ravenna and Neah from behind.

Ione shouted back, "I'm out!"

By instinct alone Astoria tossed her a full magazine. Ione slammed it home and charged the weapon. The shadowy figure spotted the new threat and began shooting from the hip towards Ione and Dayton.

"Mistake," Ione muttered and quickly shouldered the weapon. Rounds splattered across the road from their attacker and slammed into the SUV. Astoria fell to his knees as chips of asphalt struck his chest.

Ione centered the sight on the largest part of the other human, lowered her point of aim to between the knees and belt line. She flicked the firing selector to three-round burst and gently squeezed the trigger.

The first round struck the upper thigh, the second in the abdomen, and the third at the base of the neck. The figure went down backwards, spread-eagle on the shoulder of the formerly peaceful lane to a small town cemetery.

Astoria stood up, and then stepped behind Ione, as if she were an invincible shield. "Jesus, woman, are you all like this?"

199

---

Ravenna staggered out of the brush pile and leaned against the van, sagging on three flat tires. Her impromptu dressing had slipped; blood pooled and began to freeze on the asphalt of the cemetery lane. An odd noise made her twist around. A man in a wheel chair had come around the end of the van with a handgun pointed at her in one hand, and the other hand raised palm towards her, a rifle slung over his shoulder.

"Okay, little lady, I see you have power, and I'm not looking for a fight." He smiled at her.

Ravenna rested again against the van. The man's voice

was oddly familiar and reassuring. She knew this man, from, well, from somewhere, from sometime. Shadows in her vision closed in around her. She thought of a picnic as a child with her family where a nice man pushed her on the tire swing that hung from the oak tree in her parents' back yard. She sagged trying to catch her balance by reaching for the door handle, she missed.

"Okay, my buddy is coming up here in a second; he will take a look at that leg of yours. And possibly more." The man's gaze dropped to her torso.

Ravenna got a quizzical look about her. The pain in her leg and arms defused the logic of it all. She thought, what an odd thing to say until she realized that her blouse was tattered, exposing more of her than she would have wanted. She struggled to adjust it as her knees began to buckle.

A strong arm came around her waist, "Don't worry, Miss, the Boy Scouts have arrived." Budd Todd picked up Ravenna Lakota and carried her up the road. The colonel wheeled along behind them, backwards, the rifle at the ready, the motor slightly whining as it strained going up the hill.

## 200

In the distance the roar of other aircraft greeted them. A flight package of three helicopters arrived: two settled down in the cemetery and disgorged a National Guard Rifle Company from Fairchild Air Force Base. The third was a gunship which slowly worked the forest at just above the tree height. They fanned out into the forest. There was a brief exchange of gunfire in the Ponderosa woodlands. One group grabbed a Stokes basket and ran off to the south. In minutes they had recovered Neah Bey. Ione and Dayton drove down the hill, and helped Budd load Ravenna into another Stokes and then into the one of the choppers. The rotors began turning, and all useful conversation stopped as the craft lifted off and headed south.

The colonel looked at Budd and Astoria. "Well, we should be proud that we completed the mission." He pulled a large sliver flask from under his wheel chair, and then a handful of cigars. "Let's celebrate!" From either side of the clearing two camouflaged men emerged. One massive carrying a cannon, the other greyhound slim carrying a compound bow.

"Have enough for all of us?" spoke the larger of the two.

### 201

Adiba had taken splinters of stone and bullet shards in her calf muscles. It was agonizing to crawl through the underbrush to where the backup cars were hidden. When she got there, only one car remained. In the first aid kit some over-the-counter pain killers helped only slightly, and the odds and ends of the first aid kit were hardly sufficient to be of much use. It had been a long drive to Kadar's base in the Midwest. She suffered through two modest surgeries to remove metal slivers.

Adiba began filling in very interested parties from all over the world.

## 202

Haytham, one of Kadar's handpicked men, had been injured by the blast from the Barrett that toppled the tree. He pulled a splinter of pine from his left side. Haytham had been acting as spotter for the sniper Nasih. When the tree came down, it crushed his AK, bending it in a large 'U' shape. He threw it to the side. The splinters had pierced Nasih through the middle. Nasih had hardly any air left in him; as the tree crushed him, all he could do was gasp.

Haytham stumbled away and watched the helicopter fall in flames a mile from his spot. The jets made him dive for cover as they insolently did a victory roll over the cemetery and disappeared over the tree line to the south. Using the damaged scope from Nasih's rifle, he could see the van leaning on flattened tires. A man with fake legs was carrying a beautiful woman in his arms up the road, followed, of all things, by a man in a wheelchair.

A pair of helicopters landed on the cemetery and disgorged many armed men. He had seen that look before many times; Americans on the hunt in a pack were rarely beaten. Rarely. A few gunshots echoed through the forest. Haytham jogged through the forest and ran past an associate with an arrow sticking him to a tree. He was ever mindful of the air cap provided by the angry gunship.

He was at the backup cars and dove into the one closest to the road. The little sedan, unobtrusive as it was intended to be, was too low-slung for fast driving on the back roads. Haytham sped over a bump and high-centered the small car on a granite rock in the center of the road. In his anger he slammed the car in reverse and forward until free.

The damage to the underside was shortly evidenced when the oil light came on and smoke began emanating from the overheating engine.

203

Adiba had managed to make contact with the remnants of Kadar's network, pretty much left in shambles after every agency involved in anti-terrorism in the world got a free day hunting the participants down. Those that remained were very fearful, in part by the explosion of drones being operated by civilians armed with pictures of the wanted parties. Tracking terrorists had become a video game in which there were just losers.

As she drove along a back road in southern Wisconsin in the late fall, Adiba's cell phone rang. It was a brand new phone, with a new number that fewer than a dozen people in the world new of. The screen was blank, no caller ID, no company name, no heading describing a restricted number, just a blank screen. She tapped the button and said, "Yes?"

There were some faint clicks and a bit of static, and then a voice, a voice of an old man, a dry voice, like sand being poured through a rusty funnel, like ash being borne along by an errant breeze, like snake scales on dry leaves, "We have mutual enemies. I think a combined effort might be productive." And with that the phone went dead.

Adiba pulled over into an old farm field turnoff. Calmly she turned off the engine and stared at the phone. When she went to the recent call menu, there was none indicated. It was as if the call had never been received. She sat back in the seat and idly watched a murder of crows lilt across the grey sky. Biting her lower lip, she thought, *how is this possible?* She answered herself after a moment, *someone with resources.* Another moment of watching the crows and she thought, *and possibly someone who wants to see Neah Bey dead.*

## 204

The old man hung up the phone and watched a lazy trail of cigarette smoke crawl upwards. It finally got in the path of the small fan and dissipated in the room.

The room was lined with new computers and radios.

There was a knock on one of the two doors into the room. He stubbed out the cigarette with the hand that had only a finger and a thumb.

## 205

Merritt had to nearly put the truck in the ditch as the little car came around the corner, taking up half the road. A cloud of smoke poured from under the hood. Sprague opened the door and looked at his wife, "Stay here, sweetie. Let me see what this is."

Merritt shouted at Sprague, "Look out!" A man was running toward the truck with a gun aimed at her. Sprague got to the front of the truck and stopped.

"Give me your truck, and I may let your woman live!" Haytham shouted and to emphasize his intent pointed the gun into the sky and pulled the trigger.

Sprague winced in anticipation of the blast from the gun. The gun merely clicked. Before Haytham could operate the slide to load a new round, Sprague was on him.

## 206

Blanca and Padden saw the little car that was smoking drive past their car on the road to the mine. "Oh, hell, he isn't going anywhere far!" Padden shouted. Thinking that one of the valley residents was in danger, they followed the little car until it nearly collided with Merritt and Sprague's Ford.

"What is this?" Blanca shouted when an unknown man raised a gun and tried to fire it. Sprague leapt like a huge feline, descending on the man as an alley cat would dispatch a rat.

Sprague threw the man to the ground and kicked him in the ribs. Haytham tied to pull a knife from his belt sheath, but the enraged Sprague batted it away with his hand.

Padden ran to help his brother-in-law. He was struck on the side of the head, knocking him off balance. He turned to face this threat and was surprised to see a slender woman in a grey suit shaking her finger at him as one would scold a child. "No, and I mean no!" She smiled an odd lopsided smile owing to scarring on the side of her face. Angered and his face smarting, he turned toward her, hate furrowing his face.

"Not a good idea, kid." A deep voice sounded from behind him. A tall broad shouldered man with short hair smiled at Padden. "Take a chill pill."

Flanked by two unknowns, Padden looked at his wife, "Are you okay?" Blanca nodded to the affirmative.

By this time Sprague had picked up a large rock and was bashing Haytham's face. "One!" he shouted and struck the prone man. "Two!" and again the rock came down.

Tex leaned against his SUV. "This could take a while."

The slender woman said "Yes, I suppose so." She reached into her pocket and pulled out a cigarette and a lighter.

"I thought you quit that habit." Tex frowned at the woman.

In the back ground Sprague was up to "Seven!"

"Yeah, I thought so too. But, it's kind of an occupational issue I guess." She smiled at Padden and Blanca, "So you are the brother- and sister-in-law? Padden and Blanca?"

Sprague was up to "Ten!" Merritt was mesmerized by her husband's massive shoulders moving inside his shirt. The rock came up and down again, "Eleven!"

Haytham barely could raise a hand to defend himself, and when he did, Sprague merely swatted it away and brought the rock down again, "Twelve!"

"How many times is he going to do that?" Padden asked.

The slender woman took a puff and said, "As far as we are concerned, he can do that all day and most of tomorrow, but I don't think it is going to take that long."

"Thirteen! Fourteen! Fifteen!" Splatters of blood dotted Sprague's face and arms. Sweat poured from his face and soaked his shirt to the waist.

The slender woman took another puff, "I think fifteen is the magic number, what do you think, Tex?"

Tex looked at his watch and the sky, "Seems fair."

Sprague looked up in surprise at the slender woman

and the tall man. Breathing heavily from the exertion he wheezed, "I know you! You are--"

Tex put his finger up to his lips and shook his head from side to side. "No, Captain, that is still classified, and you will be held to that."

Sprague stood, equal in height and thickness to this man called Tex. "Think so, here, on my turf?"

Tex smiled, "Sprague Palmer, Captain, Delta Force, do you remember your team name?"

Sprague squared up and said, "Yes I do! We were the SCUD-Killerz." He dragged the "z" out for a second longer.

The slender woman walked over to the still form of Haytham. "You are kind of a dumbass; you know?" She drew a side arm that was equipped with a silencer. There was a slight pop, Haytham's head jolted a little. She looked closely at the corpse, "I think that was between the eyes. What do you think, Tex?"

Tex squinted at the corpse, "I need a beer and a pizza." With that he walked to the back of the SUV and pulled out two five-gallon cans. With one hand he rolled Haytham into the ditch and poured the contents of the two cans over the body.

He handed the two empty cans to Padden, "Would you mind recycling these?"

The slender woman in the grey suit looked at the still burning stub of her cigarette and with a practiced hand flicked the ember onto the corpse. It ignited ferociously, burning nearly white.

Tex got into the driver's seat, "We gotta go, Ma'am."

The slender woman shook Merritt's hand, "Have him swing by the VA, and have the doctor give Sprague a once over. However, I think your days of going to the mine are over." She gave Merritt a lopsided smile. "I think you will all be better now."

Merritt held her husband's hand, and wiped the remnants of the battle from his face with her handkerchief. "How do you know us, all this, and everything?"

Again the lopsided smile, "We know everything; it's just the way we are." She turned to the SUV.

As she walked by Padden and Blanca, "You will, of course, keep all this to yourselves? Please?"

Padden and Blanca nodded and stepped back to allow the woman access to the car. She got in and stared out the front window, lost in her own thoughts.

Tex pulled the SUV up to Sprague, "Get your head back in the game, kid, and give me a call. We always got space for the best." He smiled and said, "And in about an hour or so, would you be so kind to bury that shit over there?" He jerked his head to the nearly incinerated corpse.

Merritt stepped toward Tex with a frown, "Leave. Now. And don't hold your breath for my husband to call."

Tex smiled, "As you wish." He stepped on the gas and the SUV slid around the corner into the gathering dusk.

207

Neah recovered and was sitting in the office above the woodshed working on a report. He spent much time in physical therapy; he commented to Ravenna that each time he cheated death it seemed to take longer to heal.

Ravenna provided guidance, "That's what happens when you get old. Really old. Tragically old. So old in fact that it is just plain hard to describe how really tragically old." She ducked when Neah threw a wad of paper at her head.

In his conversations with the Smiths and Ravenna he made mention that he did not think they knew everything; parts were missing. The Smiths were alarmed about his several comments about loose ends and things left unanswered. In time, he accepted the state of affairs and began working on other assignments.

## 208

Neah Bey sat in the woodshed's second-floor office. The triple-glazed windows and extra thick insulation made it virtually an island of silence. He sat and stared across the intervening space between him and Ravenna.

Had he another life, he could easily have fallen for her. Jet black hair, a figure belonging to a very muscular cheerleader, but there was that temper to be cautious of. Years before bad guys tried to cut Ione out of traffic. Ravenna led the security over-flight of a four-person team. All Ione could remember was that it seemed like a traffic accident had happened to one side of her and slightly behind. It was not an accident.

One of the potential kidnappers was shot in the face as a way of inspiring the other. It was only partially successful. The survivor was confused about the severity of his position. After pulling out his fingernails with a Leatherman tool, Ravenna gave him an option: die horribly, or just plain die. He chose very poorly by refusing to relinquish information freely and was made to suffer for it. He was exposed to the anger of Ravenna for three days until it was determined that his brain had stopped working due to extreme pain and neural overload. Ravenna drove an ice pick into his ear as insurance.

Neah was grateful that Ravenna was on his side. The information gathered by Ravenna and her team was most useful. He was very glad that Ravenna and Ione hit it off and had become friends, in spite of the disparity in their ages. They elected to keep the full details of the incident between them, lest it weigh on Ione's conscious.

## 209

Dr. Astoria sat back in his small apartment. The wall had been repaired, the damaged bookcase replaced. In the meantime, he had been to Omaha and picked up the contents of the safety deposit box. Assured by the Smiths, and the redoubtable Ravenna Lakota, that all surveillance equipment had been removed, he felt comforted. He was leaving in a few days, heading back to the ice he loved so much. Everett Pierce signed on as the second in command.

He sipped from his beer and looked over his few possessions. Most were going to be given away to local charities or needy students. His newest addition hung from the wall. While not remnants of the Shackleton, Scott, or really any expedition of note, the snow goggles were in great condition for their age. He had one of his friends in the college fine arts program make a special shadow box to display the goggles in a fitting manner. The museum-grade glass that protected the artifact was particularly stout.

He did not think the frame for the goggles was too ornate, as it highlighted the contents rather than overpowered them. The frame itself was also stout; made from wood Astoria had scavenged from an abandoned whaling station they had sheltered near on one expedition.

As was his custom, Dr. Dayton Astoria updated his will before heading out to Antarctica. With no living relatives, this was an easy process. Some of his unique pieces would go to the museum at Central Washington University, some personal tools to Pierce, the money to scholarship funds at the University of Wisconsin. He stared at the goggles and made a special note for them. If he perished on this trip, the goggles would go to Ione Bey.

He knew that Neah would be curious and closely examine the frame. He laughed out loud; tears welled in his eyes as he continued to laugh. Neah thought he knew it all. The Smiths thought they knew it all.

But only Astoria and Sloan Bucoda did know it all.

It would be the cosmic joke of all time. He laughed more. Dr. Dayton Astoria was grateful that Neah and his associates had saved his life and given him the opportunity to continue his work.

Astoria wondered what Neah's expression would be when he took apart the frame and found the other one third of the Antikythera Mechanism; except his parts of the Mechanism were in pristine condition.

210

The Sister opened the mail and began sorting the few checks that were donations and the much larger stack of bills. Some bills were well past their due dates. The power and water bills were opened first; bank accounts for

230

checking and the laughable savings account were usually opened last.

She stopped and stared at the water bill up until now they had not paid it for nine months, and here it said that it had a credit balance. In fact, it had a credit of several thousands of dollars.

"Well, that just can't be right." That bill was placed off to the side. She then opened the power bill, also left unpaid for nearly a year now. It showed a credit as well, a credit of enough money to pay for the power consumption for the next year.

The Sister sat down and stared at the two bills. This was impossible. This had to be a mistake.

Out of curiosity, she opened the bank statements.

They came running from various parts of the convent and the surrounding fields of early spring plantings. The shouts and laughter were uncommon in the convent.

She sat on the floor of the small office, laughing hysterically and crying at the same time. The only phone the convent used was dangling off the hook, a tiny voice shouting, "Hello? Hello? Is everything all right? This is the bank, is everything all right? Hello?"

The petit elder Sister with the emotionless eyes picked up the phone and placed it back on the cradle. She then reached down and took the power, water, and bank statements from the semi-lucid Sister now laughing loudly.

She read over them, and had the faintest glimmer of a smile cross her face. Silesia came into the room and her gaze shifted from the seated woman to the elder woman. The other Sisters were in amazement, alternating between thoughtful thanks and laughter.

The elder woman passed the papers over to Silesia.

"You have powerful friends." Silesia took the papers and quickly scanned the data.

"Yes, they are. With your permission I would like to call them and tell them thank you." Silesia asked.

To everyone's surprise the elder Sister said, "Oh, hell yes!"

## 211

Ravenna noticed him staring rather blankly in the general area of her belt buckle. "Hello? Anyone home?" Before Bey could answer his computer chirped, indicating an incoming email.

"I was just thinking about things." He turned to the screen. "Hmm, maybe you better watch this. Could be important."

Ravenna leaned forward, "Why should I read your emails?" She asked.

Neah rolled his chair back, "Well, because it's from the girl in the coma, Ruby La Push." Neah clicked on the message icon.

The screen blanked to snow. "Oh, crap!" Neah stared at the screen thinking he had just infected the entire Smith network with a virus. The snowy image along with the sound of the static faded; an image began to emerge from the snow. It was Ruby La Push.

She stared at the camera, eyes unblinking, only the very slight rise and fall of her shoulders indicated that she was even breathing. Neah tensed, not knowing what to do, not knowing whom to call. Ravenna's hand resting on his shoulder began to crush his trapezius.

232

Ruby La Push winked at the camera, swallowed, and began.

"Hello, Mr. Bey, my name is Ruby La Push. I think it is fair to say at this point that I am dead and you are getting this message days, weeks, maybe months from when I started my program." Bey hit the pause button.

Neah looked over his shoulder at Ravenna, his right hand dropping to the grip of the .45, spooked by the image and voice before him. He turned to the cameras watching over the house and felt more at ease in seeing that Ione was in her quilting room pushing cats out of the way of her fabric cutting. All was normal.

Ravenna speed dialed the agent at the hospital to check on Ruby's condition; she was breathing on her own, and responding feebly to external stimuli. The agent said there was a bit of a scuffle at the hospital, and there was going to have to be some major paperwork written as they had to Taser a guy in a wheelchair who tried to barge into Ruby's room.

Bey hit play again.

"I am sorry if this bothers you, but I have a story to tell. And it all starts with what Doctor Astoria found." Again she paused, staring into the camera, into the eyes of the agents that had seen everything before; everything except this. The image of Ruby took a breath and continued, "You see, I looked over his shoulder and watched him examine the, well, the artifacts." She appeared to look down and read from some prepared notes, or briefly study a computer monitor, "There were strange markings on them. Astoria tried to figure it out, but he just used the wrong logic."

Ravenna whispered, "I have to tell you this is freaking

me out, a whole lot." Her grip on Bey's shoulder was beyond painful.

Ruby smiled. "Well, I guess I'm just smarter than Doctor Dayton Astoria." She laughed softly for a moment. "I have been running a cipher-breaking program along with many other linguistic and fuzzy logic programs on the markings Dr. Astoria discovered on the artifacts. Here is the result. Mr. Bey? I do hope you are sitting down."

Slowly it came across the screen,

"A-t-l-a-n-t-i-s"